Acting Edition

I0591875

Follow Me to Nellie's

by Dominique Morisseau

FOR PRODUCTION INQUIRIES

UNITED STATES AND CANADA
info@concordtheatricals.com
1-866-979-0447

UNITED KINGDOM AND EUROPE
licensing@concordtheatricals.co.uk
020-7054-7200

Each title is subject to availability from Concord Theatricals Corp., depending upon country of performance. Please be aware that FOLLOW ME TO NELLIE'S may not be licensed by Concord Theatricals Corp. in your territory. Professional and amateur producers should contact the nearest Concord Theatricals Corp. office or licensing partner to verify availability.

No one shall make any changes in this title(s) for the purpose of production. No part of this book may be reproduced, stored in a retrieval system, scanned, uploaded, or transmitted in any form, by any means, now known or yet to be invented, including mechanical, electronic, digital, photocopying, recording, videotaping, or otherwise, without the prior written permission of the publisher. No one shall share this title(s), or any part of this title(s), through any social media or file hosting websites.

For all inquiries regarding motion picture, television, online/digital and other media rights, please contact Concord Theatricals Corp.

MUSIC AND THIRD-PARTY MATERIALS USE NOTE

Licensees are solely responsible for obtaining formal written permission from copyright owners to use copyrighted music and/or other copyrighted third-party materials (e.g., artworks, logos) in the performance of this play and are strongly cautioned to do so. If no such permission is obtained by the licensee, then the licensee must use only original music and materials that the licensee owns and controls. Licensees are solely responsible and liable for clearances of all third-party copyrighted materials, including without limitation music, and shall indemnify the copyright owners of the play(s) and their licensing agent, Concord Theatricals Corp., against any costs, expenses, losses and liabilities arising from the use of such copyrighted third-party materials by licensees. For music, please contact the appropriate music licensing authority in your territory for the rights to any incidental music.

IMPORTANT BILLING AND CREDIT REQUIREMENTS

If you have obtained performance rights to this title, please refer to your licensing agreement for important billing and credit requirements.

FOLLOW ME TO NELLIE'S was first produced by Premiere Stages (John J. Wooten, Producing Artistic Director) at the Kean University Zella Fry Theatre in Union, New Jersey on July 14, 2011. The performance was directed by John J. Wooten, with sets by Joseph Gourley, costumes by Karen Hart, lights by Nadine Charlson, and sound by Charles Lawlor. The cast was as follows:

NELLIE (AINEE)....................................Lynda Graváttá

NA ROSE ....Kelly McCreary

MARLA..Nyahale Allie

REE ANN ....Michelle Wilson

SANDY .... Ley Smith

OSSIE ....Warner Miller

ROLLO ....Harold Surrat

TOM JR. .... Adam Couperthwaite

FOLLOW ME TO NELLIE'S was the 2011 Play Festival Winner of the Premiere Play Festival at Premiere Stages.

CHARACTERS

NELLIE (AINEE) – (Late 50s) Black woman, strong, unflinching, and stern, with a hidden capacity to love deeply. The Madame of the Whorehouse.

NA ROSE – (19) Black woman, beautiful yet awkward, soft, fragile, lyrical, and unsure of herself. An aspiring blueswoman.

MARLA – (Late 20s / early 30s) Black woman, saucy, sexy, voluptuous, troubled, and vulgar. One of the "gals."

REE ANN – (Mid-late 30s) Black woman, sensible, steady, dedicated, and unyielding. One of the "gals."

SANDY – (Early 20s) Black woman, sweet, stunning, spirited, fun-loving, optimistic, and extremely sexual. One of the "gals."

OSSIE – (Early 20s) Black man, handsome, proud, charming, strong, and confident. A freedom fighter.

ROLLO – (50s) Black man, nervous energy, jittery, talkative, and lovable. Nellie's oldest friend.

TOM JR. – (Early 20s) White man, handsome, friendly, and eager. An aspiring do-gooder with a troubled heart. Son of the Sheriff.

SETTING

At the infamous Nellie Jackson's Whorehouse.

Natchez, Mississippi.

TIME

1955. The beginning of June. Hot and humid.

PLAYWRIGHT'S NOTE

Nellie Jackson's Whorehouse was a real and famous place in Natchez, Mississippi. This story is based in part on my beloved aunt, Ms. Nellie Jackson (called Ainee by her family), a well-loved woman in the community who was known more for her "heart of gold" and the way in which she would take care of people in the community than for the mere fact that she was a Madame. She could pass for White. Casting for Nellie can be open for all shades and complexions of Black women, but when casting lighter complexioned women, please keep in the language that reveals her color. Otherwise, such lines may be cut.

ACT I

Prologue

(A red and white awning hangs over the down right apron of the stage sheltering a screen door.)

*(Lights up on beautiful young woman, **NA ROSE**. Knitting in her hands. She stares at a jukebox.)*

NA ROSE.
> FOLLOW... FOLLOW IT...*

> *(Headlights from a truck beam onto stage, and crossfade into an ominous light rising on a man in his late fifties, **ROLLO**. He is frantic and hasty.)*

ROLLO. *(Calling in a whisper.)* Lil' Bit?! They's comin'. You ready?

NA ROSE. *(Oblivious.)*
> HEAR THAT BLUES AND... FOLLOW IT...

ROLLO. *(Persistent.)* We got to get on outta here, Lil' Bit. Quick!

> *(The ominous light moves over **NA ROSE**.)*

NA ROSE.

>TO A PLACE WITH DRINK AND AILS.

>>*(Another ominous light rises on a beautiful woman in her fifties,* **NELLIE JACKSON,** *in a rocking chair, creaking to and fro.)*

NELLIE. Don't get swooped up in the wrong winds, Rose. I worry 'bout you.

NA ROSE.

>TO A PLACE WITH GHOSTS AND WAILS

>>*(Another ominous light rises on a young man,* **OSSIE.***)*

OSSIE. You ever been up north?

ROLLO. Got to go, Lil' Bit. Got to go'on now.

NA ROSE.

>TO A PLACE WHERE DREAMS SET SAIL

NELLIE. The blues ain't nothin' but heartache and despair.

OSSIE. You can be all those things you've been dreaming.

>>*(***NA ROSE** *stares at* **ROLLO,** *who is twitching nervously. She stares at* **OSSIE.** *She stares at* **NELLIE.***)*

NA ROSE.

>HEAR THAT BLUES AND...

NELLIE. *(Softly.)* You the one I can make it right for, Rose. And I'm gonna.

>>*(A bright light blazes the stage. A flame. It illuminates* **NA ROSE, NELLIE, OSSIE,** *and* **ROLLO.** *Then flame out. All are gone except* **NA ROSE.***)*

NA ROSE.

>FOLLOW IT...

(A final ominous light washes over a jukebox. Brighter than the others. **NA ROSE** *clings to it desperately. Kisses it and it magically plays a tune*. She looks at it with surprise.)*

(The sound of a truck begins. **NA ROSE** *looks after it...uncertainly... Lights fade...)*

---

* A license to produce *Follow Me to Nellie's* does not include a performance license for any third-party or copyrighted music. Licensees should create an original composition or use music in the public domain. For further information, please see the Music and Third Party Materials Use Note on page iii.

Scene One

(Lights up on a common room inside Nellie Jackson's whorehouse. A grand jukebox sits in the center of the room and is the main attraction. Supporting features are the surrounding couches with plastic covering and fancy lace doilies and an antique rocking chair reserved especially as a throne for **NELLIE.***)*

(To the left of the common room is a small kitchenette. A table in a corner sits with a lace tablecloth and decorated chairs. A cabinet rests across from the table. The rest of the kitchen is unseen.)

*(***NA ROSE*** sits in the background and watches as* **SANDY, MARLA,** *and* **REE ANN** *dance around the room while a song like Elmore James' "Dust My Broom"* blares from the speakers of the jukebox.)*

REE ANN. Oooo Marla, turn that up! Can't it go no louder?

MARLA. Don't turn up. Ain't got no knobs.

SANDY. I think I'ma find this man and marry him. Won't he make a good husband?

REE ANN. *(Laughing.)* Sandy, just cuz you yella don't mean Elmore James gonna marry you!

---

* A license to produce *Follow Me to Nellie's* does not include a performance license for "Dust My Broom." The publisher and author suggest that the licensee contact ASCAP or BMI to ascertain the music publisher and contact such music publisher to license or acquire permission for performance of the song. If a license or permission is unattainable for "Dust My Broom," the licensee may not use the song in *Follow Me to Nellie's* but should create an original composition in a similar style or use a similar song in the public domain. For further information, please see the Music and Third Party Materials Use Note on page iii.

SANDY. You so color struck Ree Ann. I'm talking about somethin' deeper. Just listen to that guitar. He plays it so it goes deep down inside a you and makes you feel like consummating somethin' with him.

REE ANN. Ain't nothin' deeper than color.

MARLA. Gimme another nickel. Thang only take nickels.

REE ANN. I ain't got another nickel. That was my last one. Why you ain't got no pieces? Didn't Charlie do you right?

MARLA. Charlie did me just fine. It's Sammy that got off cheap.

SANDY. Oooo Marla. You ain't 'spose to be lettin' 'em off cheap. Nellie gon' git you again.

MARLA. I ain't worried about Nellie. Ol' bat a have to see good first. Long as I keep her specs hidden, she gon' keep thinkin' them pennies is dimes…and you ain't gon' tell her one thang different, Lil' Bit.

(NA ROSE looks at MARLA, accosted.)

REE ANN. Marl, stop pointin' fingers.

MARLA. Everybody know Lil' Bit over there is Nellie's lil' con-fee-dant *("Confidant.")*. Tell her everythang. What's goin' on on the moon? Just ask Lil' Bit over there. *(Beat / mumbling.)* She best just stay outta Marl's business and get some business of her own…

REE ANN. Go'on and quit your fussin' already.

(NA ROSE buries herself in her knitting.)

MARLA. What you over there knittin', Lil' Bit?

NA ROSE. Sweater.

MARLA. What happened to Marla's shawl you was 'spose to be finishing? I gave you fifty cents nearly a whole week ago.

NA ROSE. I'm almost done with it. Had to wait 'til I got more yarn. Ainee 'spose to be gettin' me some from Tillie's today.

MARLA. Well I ain't waiting forever, ya know. Marla ain't got to wait on nobody. I need somethin' new and fancy to wear for when Jim come back to get me.

REE ANN. Oh Marla, please not another Jim story.

MARLA. Ain't no story. This is truth.

REE ANN. Truth or no truth, keep it to yaself.

MARLA. When you got a man like Jim you holdin' on for, you don't keep it to yaself. You open up yo' mouth and speak all his goodness to the world. And keep a lil' of his smell in you *(Points to her crotch.)* so you remember who it really belongs to.

SANDY. *(Disgusted.)* Marla please...

MARLA. Oh please yaself. Got me a good man gone off to service in that Germany, and soon as he gets discharged, he comin' back for me and we gon' get married and I'm gettin' outta here for good.

REE ANN. Huh! Who gone marry a whore?

MARLA. *(Plainly.)* Jim.

REE ANN. Marla, Jim done left and ain't comin' back here. And I'm gettin' sick and tired of you lyin' to everybody.

MARLA. If I'm lyin', I'm dyin'.

REE ANN. Well I'll see you at the funeral.

SANDY. I wants to hear another tune.

NA ROSE. Here – I got a nickel. What's your pick?

SANDY. I could use a lil' bit o' some John Lee Hooker right now.

> *(**NA ROSE** goes over to the jukebox and searches for the song.)*

(John Lee Hooker's "Sugar Mama" plays.*
SANDY*'s hips begin to sway as if on their*
own...)

Love the way down home blues like to get inside of your
hips and make you feel like rollin' 'em. Nothin' more
satisfyin' than the sound of a guitar. 'Specially in a man's
arms. Way he hold it like he hold a woman. Pluckin' it
with each finger... *(Suddenly pensive.)* I been a guitar
befo'...yessir I has...and it felt good gettin' played...

NA ROSE. For me it's the words.

SANDY. The words? What about 'em?

NA ROSE. Put together like fabric. Like knittin' without the
yarn. Way somebody carefully weave words together
to make you feel like they just in yo' size. That's some
kinda blues magic.

REE ANN. Well I just like the sound filling up the house,
so when ya'll get to talkin' silly and carryin' on like this,
I can just tune you both right on out.

SANDY. Oh Ree Ann! You always just so particular. Can't
tell the difference between you and Nellie half the time.

REE ANN. We need to get to cleanin' this place 'fore she get
home from church.

NA ROSE. She 'sposin' to stop downtown first with Rollo.
New Sheriff wanna meet with her.

REE ANN. Thas right. Folk sayin' that new Sheriff move
here with his son. Widowed, they say. 'Spose to got a

---

different attitude 'bout Colored folk than most Whites.

SANDY. Ain't soundin' like it. Way he put Eli Perkins in that jail.

REE ANN. That Eli Perkins done a fool thang. Comin' back down here with some school fella to try and get Negroes votin'. He oughta knows better. Don't know what happened to the other one. His partner.

MARLA. Say that other one done took off and hiding from the law.

SANDY. I shoul' hope he done went back north. Thang's bad for northern Negroes coming back down. Like that young fella over in Money from Chicago. Still can't get him outta my head.

MARLA. Way they found him over in the Tallahatchie...

REE ANN. *(Shaking her head with memory.)* That picture in the paper... Lawd.

SANDY. Still give me the creeps. I been dreamin' 'bout him. What he looked like before them mens put that hurtin' on him. That one picture of him smilin' next to the one where he... *(Shift.)* Lawd, I wouldna been able to stand seein' him up close and personal in that open casket. Picture make it like somebody squeezed his face 'til it like to pop on one side. That ain't a way to treat no fella. 'Specially a young. Fourteen.

MARLA. He was a handsome fella, too – that Emmet Till. Bettin' if that gal he whistled at ain't have her husband around, she'd a been all kinds of flattered. I done seen these White gals lookin' at Negro mens, then pretendin' they wunn't. I tellin' you.

REE ANN. Well these other northern fellas betta not be bringin' that same kinda thang over here to Natchez. Eli Perkins and that other one – whatever his name be –

NA ROSE. Heard tell it Ossie Brown.

REE ANN. Well that Ossie Brown be in a heap of trouble if he ever get caught. These Southern boys go up north and act like they don't know the first thang 'bout bein' Negro when they come back down. Natchez ain't the place for that kinda ambition. They ain't nothin' but trouble.

SANDY. I like a lil' trouble in a man. Makes him excitin'.

MARLA. Long as he ain't got trouble with his tools. That ain't excitin' at all.

REE ANN. Marla, don't be speakin' indecent right now.

NA ROSE. Negroes votin', that'd be somethin' if it could happen, wouldn't it? Be real prideful.

REE ANN. Na Rose hush up that kinda talk. What it matter 'bout pride? Go'on hand me that broom and let's get to cleanin' 'fore Nellie get back.

> (**NA ROSE** *nods and heads over to the jukebox to insert the coin, but stops immediately when she hears:)*

NELLIE. *(Offstage.)* Rose?! Rooooooossssssseeeee!!! Come open this back gate for Ainee, sugar!

> (*The women all freeze and look at each other wildly.* **NA ROSE** *runs offstage toward* **NELLIE.***)*

> (*The women quickly unplug the juke box and scramble around the room, pretending to be cleaning.* **SANDY** *picks up a Bible from an end table.)*

> (*Enter* **NELLIE JACKSON**. *She wears a fancy hat and dressy gloves and is dressed to the nines.* **ROLLO** *follows in after her.)*

SANDY. And in Revelations: 15; Verse: 4, God said –

NELLIE. Don't even try to con me Sandy. I know ya'll wasn't in here learnin' the word.

ROLLO. Gig is up Sandy. Go'on put that Bible down 'fore the lightnin strike it out yo' hands.

> (**NELLIE** *scans the room and walks over to the jukebox. The women watch her nervously. She picks up the unplugged cord.*)

NELLIE. Still hot. This best not mean what I think it means. I done told ya'll about this box. It ain't for play. For customers only.

SANDY. We was just testin' it out. Makin' sure it works for you.

NELLIE. Sandy you know better than to lie to me. Now I mean it. Don't go playin' 'round on this thang. This a brand new box Rollo brought us straight from the Trade Shop.

ROLLO. It's a beaut, too. Sold it to me for a case of Bourbon. Say it got spirits in it so the last owner let it go real cheap like. I say it got spirits alright. Spirits of the blues. We know how to turn that into somethin'...so I picked up and there it go.

NELLIE. Well it's a good way to keep money flowin' when the boys come with a truck load a friends who can't afford the merchandise. Can't afford to have it broke cuz ya'll wanna sit around here and pretend you down at the Blues Shack. Hear me?

SANDY. Yes, Nellie. I hear ya.

REE ANN. What's the new sheriff like?

ROLLO. Seem like a right fella. Call him Sheriff Toms. Real ol'-schooled but real polite-like. Even took off his hat to greet us.

REE ANN. White man tippin' his hat to a Negro?

ROLLO. Thas what he done.

MARLA. That sound suspect to me. I ain't never trusted no manners on no White folks.

ROLLO. Well he gots somethin' fo' us to worry 'bout. He ain't too keen on Nellie just yet.

NELLIE. Wants to see my books. Say it routine, but I knows what it is. That Sheriff Toms know folks done got to me 'bout Eli. Got his mama and his grandmama all the way from the north, and half the Negroes in the county ringin' me up and askin' me to get Eli outta that jail. I go down there to talk to him and he sayin' he wants to see my books.

REE ANN. Ain't you gonna be able to post his bail, Nellie?

NELLIE. Ain't sho' yet. If'n that Sheriff Toms can find any trail of paper that shows how we makes our money, he gon' shut us down. I been operatin' for twenty some odd years. And new Sheriff wants to see my books. I ain't goin' down just so easy.

SANDY. What ya gon do Nellie?

NELLIE. Gon' find what his tastes are and satisfy 'em. Gon' find what his rages are and stay clear of 'em. Like I always done.

ROLLO. My friends downtown say he's a Bourbon man.

NELLIE. That so? Let's contact our friends in Louisiana. See if we can't pick up a lil' somethin'.

ROLLO. Hear-tell the Natchez Indians lookin' to get theyselves a new stadium built. Say our new Sheriff be a huge baseball fan.

NELLIE. Well then...sounds like him an' me gots a lot in common. See what we can do 'bout that baseball stadium fund. Maybe we finds a way to get on that Sheriff's good side after all.

ROLLO. And 'member we still gots to talk about that lil' favor I'm needin' from you.

NELLIE. Sho' Rollo. We talk about it later...

(**NELLIE** *coughs. It jars her for a moment.*)

REE ANN. Gettin' a lil' cough Nellie?

(*Quickly tries to brush it off.*)

NELLIE. I'm fine. Where's Rose?

REE ANN. Must be busy makin' that shawl for Marla.

NELLIE. Marla pay her a piece yet?

MARLA. Fifty cents already.

NELLIE. Then where's my board?

(**MARLA** *looks at the women nervously.*)

MARLA. Now Nellie Jackson...you know I paid you my board already.

NELLIE. Board is two dollars and twenty-five cents a week. You think I don't know the difference between dimes and pennies, but I know you ain't been payin' me my full rent. And I know you been hidin' my specs!

MARLA. Board a be a whole lot cheaper split four ways 'steada three.

NELLIE. (*Sternly.*) Rose don't pay board.

MARLA. She gettin' plenty old. Don't you think it's 'bout time she start earnin' her keep like the rest of us?

NELLIE. (*More sternly.*) Like I say... Rose don't pay board. Rose don't trick.

MARLA. (*Pushing.*) Well how she gon' earn her keep?

NELLIE. She done already earned her keep with me a long time ago. It's my house Marl, and you don't like it, you can go'on right back down by the riverboat to do your business.

(**NA ROSE** *enters cautiously...overhearing the argument.*)

NA ROSE. Ainee, we still goin' over to Tillie's? I need to get some more yarn to finish that shawl for Marla.

NELLIE. Oh, right... I'm gon' get outta these Sunday clothes and we run over. How that sound, sugar?

MARLA. *(Answering for* **ROSE** *– sarcastically.)* Sound real sweet.

SANDY. *(Hitting her.)* Marla!

NA ROSE. Sound fine Ainee. Sound fine.

NELLIE. Good. *(Beat.)* It's a hot one today. Rollo, can you go'on down the street for me and get us some ice for the freezer?

ROLLO. Sure thang, Nellie.

NELLIE. Gals, house need straightenin'.

SANDY. Sure thang Nellie.

> *(***ROLLO*** exits.* **NELLIE** *exits.* **MARLA** *stares at* **SANDY***.)*

MARLA. *(Mockingly.)* Sure thang Nellie.

REE ANN. Marla, you gon' git enough a pushin' her buttons.

MARLA. Her buttons need a lil' pushin'.

REE ANN. You gon' learn not to bite the hand that feeds you.

MARLA. Marla don't need nobody to feeds her. Marla feeds herself! Everybody always actin' like Nellie Jackson somethin' to be thankful for all the time. That woman ain't hardly nobody's saint.

SANDY. But Natchez loves her. Whole town...'cept for you Marl. Po-lice. Priests. Nuns. Bankers. You be mighty lonely out there makin' yourself a enemy of Miss Nellie Jackson.

MARLA. Well leave me 'lone then. I'll be by my lonesome 'til Jim come back on. He all the good company I need.

(The women ignore this comment and commence to cleaning. NA ROSE lifts up pillows and searches for something under the couch.)

NA ROSE. Anybody seen a piece of parchment?

SANDY. Parchment for what?

NA ROSE. Had set it down in my room, I thought. But didn't see it just now.

REE ANN. Well we 'spose to be cleanin' up so we'll keep a eye out for it.

NA ROSE. I can help clean.

MARLA. Oh no. Please don't. We just loves cleanin' up yo' mess. Next time, leave some pee around for us so's we can clean that up too.

NA ROSE. I wouldn't –

REE ANN. Ignore her, please. She ain't got one bit a good sense today.

NA ROSE. Marla, you gonna really like what I'm doin' with that shawl. Gonna be lookin' real sassy for Jim when he come back around.

(MARLA perks up – slightly.)

MARLA. How sassy?

NA ROSE. Little Esther-sassy. Finest lady this side of the Mississippi Delta...

(Singing her own tune.)

IN A SHAWL WRAPPED 'ROUND ALL A YO' TALKIN' CURVES
AND ROCKIN' HIPS – MAKE EVERY MISSISSIPPI MAN
TWICE LICK HIS LIPS.˙

---

* A license to produce *Follow Me to Nellie's* does not include a performance license for any third-party or copyrighted music. Licensees should create an original melody. For further information, please see the Music and Third Party Materials Use Note on page iii.

MARLA. *(Beaming.)* Oooo Lil' Bit. I like how you sang that one.

SANDY. Oooo Na Rose! I loves yo' voice! You make that sound better than how a man sang it.

NA ROSE. *(Laughing.)* Well ya'll be sho' to keep an eye out for that parchment for me, won't ya?

SANDY. Sure thang. What's on it?

NA ROSE. Just a lil' somethin'.

MARLA. Somethin' like what?

NA ROSE. Lil' piece of nothin' really. Just words.

REE ANN. Like knittin' notes or somethin'?

NA ROSE. Or somethin'...

> *(**NA ROSE** is curiously vague. **SANDY** eyes her.)*

SANDY. You got a secret! Oooooo! Come on! Tell!

NA ROSE. Sandy now – I can't just yet.

SANDY. Come on, tell! It's just us. Only folks we'd tell be each other. Come on now!

NA ROSE. Well...

> *(**SANDY** grabs **NA ROSE** by the arm and pulls her to the couch. **NA ROSE** bursts with excitement.)*

I gots me a contract!

SANDY. Contract for what?

REE ANN. You mean like a workin' contract?

NA ROSE. Legal papers. This band at the Shack... Junior's Jukes...they's goin' all around the South. To Tennessee and Louisiana. Even Alabama and Florida. Want me to come with 'em. Sing for 'em. Be the lead...

SANDY. Woooweee!!! You ain't kiddin'?

NA ROSE. Naw. It's truth. Just got it from 'em last night. Been sangin' at the Shack some off nights and they say they been hearin' me. Lookin' for somebody just like me.

REE ANN. You done told Nellie 'bout this? You goin' off with some band?

NA ROSE. Not yet. Gon' tell her soon. When I get the right time. So don't ya'll say nothin' to her 'fore I can, 'kay?

MARLA. Gon' tell her befo' or after you tell her 'bout my board bein' short?

REE ANN. Marla.

MARLA. Naw naw, Ree Ann. This here's a simple question.

NA ROSE. Whatcha want from me, Marl?

MARLA. Be real simple like. You keep my secrets, I keep yours. Lessen' you wants Nellie to hear 'bout yo' contract from the likes of me. I'm sho' she'd love bein' the last to know her lil' stainless angel gon' take off on the road with some boys halfway cross the south and leave her to manage her books on her lonesome. Sho' she'd love hearin' that from me.

SANDY. Marl, you bein' low-down.

MARLA. I'm bein' necessary. Tha's what a woman like me got to be. Now...what ya say to that, Lil' Bit? We gots a deal?

NELLIE. *(Offstage.)* Rose! Fetch my hat and purse for me, sugar! Time to get to Tillie's!

MARLA. Well, sugar?

NA ROSE. Deal Marl. Deal.

MARLA. Well then, I'm guessin' I should probably give you this.

(**MARLA** *reaches in her bosom and hands*
NA ROSE *the parchment. The women look at
her incredulously.*)

What?!

(**NA ROSE** *grabs the parchment, shakes her
head, and runs off.*)

SANDY. Better go grab us a broom. (*Beat / mumbling in
disapproval.*) Marla...

(**SANDY** *exits.* **REE ANN** *shakes the couch
pillows.* **MARLA** *approaches her sweetly.*)

MARLA. Ree Ann, I needs to ask you a favor.

REE ANN. You can borrow two dollars and twenty-five cents
for board, Marl. But I'm gittin' it back with interest.

MARLA. Interest? Ain't that 'bout nothin'. Gone rob me
blind too?

REE ANN. Go'on git the duster, will you?

MARLA. I'm goin'...

(**MARLA** *exits.* **REE ANN** *looks around the
room, wipes her finger under a lampshade.
Lights fade on* **REE ANN** *staring at the dust
on her finger and shaking her head.*)

Scene Two

(Lights up on the empty common room. Out front on the apron, headlights from a car emerge. The faint sound of John Lee Hooker's "One Bourbon, One Scotch, One Beer"* is heard. A car engine roars. Suddenly, in staccato, all three elements disappear. Car engine stops. Music stops. Headlights off.)

(A double set of car doors close. Keys jangle. Footsteps emerge.)

ROLLO. *(Offstage.)* Come on in...right this way...

(ROLLO walks into view and opens the door to Nellie's. A young man enters cautiously behind him. This is OSSIE BROWN. He is as neat as possible, though his clothes are a bit tattered.)

Now you just come on in here...keep yo' manners about you. She's real big on 'em. Make sho' you gets that.

(OSSIE looks around the common room. Inhales its grandeur.)

She must out back. I'm gon' fetch her. You just stay right here. Sit anywheres you like...

(OSSIE goes to sit in the rocking chair.)

---

* A license to produce *Follow Me to Nellie's* does not include a performance license for "One Bourbon, One Scotch, One Beer." The publisher and author suggest that the licensee contact ASCAP or BMI to ascertain the music publisher and contact such music publisher to license or acquire permission for performance of the song. If a license or permission is unattainable for "One Bourbon, One Scotch, One Beer," the licensee may not use the song in *Follow Me to Nellie's* but should create an original composition in a similar style or use a similar song in the public domain. For further information, please see the Music and Third Party Materials Use Note on page iii.

Except right there! That's her chair. She ain't too keen on nobody takin' the most important seat in the house. But you can sit anywheres else.

OSSIE. Maybe I'll just stand.

ROLLO. You just wants to stay on her good side. That's all.

*(A cough heard offstage. **NELLIE** enters, struggling through it.)*

NELLIE. Rollo that you? I was gon' ask you to run me over to the pharmacy –

*(**NELLIE** stops when she sees **OSSIE**. Immediately stern.)*

ROLLO. Nellie I was just comin' to get you. Need to talk with you real important like.

NELLIE. Who's this fella?

OSSIE. Greetings, ma'am. I'm –

ROLLO. This a good friend of mine. We needs to have a chat, you an' me.

NELLIE. Right now? I had some thangs to tend to –

ROLLO. It's somethin' pretty urgent, Nellie. Right now.

*(**NELLIE** looks at **ROLLO** – his sincerity.)*

NELLIE. Alright then...

(She motions them over to the couch.)

(Yelling.) Ree Ann, come bring me three glasses of water!

REE ANN. *(Offstage.)* Sure thang, Nellie!

(She walks importanty over to her chair.)

NELLIE. Now, what's this about urgent?

ROLLO. Nellie, this here is my young friend, Mr. Ossie Brown.

(**OSSIE** *bows his head to* **NELLIE**.)

OSSIE. Pleasure, ma'am.

NELLIE. Ossie Brown? The one what come down with Eli to get Negroes voting? One who hidin' from the law?

OSSIE. Yes, ma'am, that's –

ROLLO. That's him Nellie.

NELLIE. What you doin' bringing him here? You know what kinda mark this fella got on him?

ROLLO. That's what I need to talk to you 'bout. Ossie here in trouble. Come all the way down with Eli from that school up there in Washington D.C.

OSSIE. Howard University –

ROLLO. And he's been doin' real good studyin' the law and politics and that fancy stuff –

OSSIE. Education major actually, but I got involved in –

ROLLO. Lots of stuff dealin' with that there Council with all the Important Negroes in Belzoni –

OSSIE. The RCNL –

ROLLO. And the folks are sayin' this Council's done some real stuff in Mississippi. Done got thirty-some of the Blacks in Humphreys County registered to vote. Ain't that somethin'?

NELLIE. Didn't that reverend get hisself shot out there? One what did that?

ROLLO. Yes, Nellie...that's so. But don't change what he done. And my friend, Ossie here...well, him and Eli come to Natchez to pick up the torch. Come to teach our people how to pass them registration tests.

NELLIE. Mr. Brown... I done heard about your business

here. That Eli Perkins got some family in Jackson. They been ringin' me left and right to help post bail for him. He's in a tough rut with the law right now.

OSSIE. Yes ma'am, I know –

ROLLO. He know that, Nellie.

NELLIE. And now you in trouble the same. Thinkin' maybe it's time for you to head back up north, ain't it?

OSSIE. Well, no ma'am –

ROLLO. Nellie, Ossie still here cuz the job ain't finished. Registration deadline in one week. He need to stay 'til then.

NELLIE. Another week? You still tryin' to finish this?

OSSIE. Yes ma'am, I am.

NELLIE. Mr. Brown, you ain't heard about what happened to that northern young'un over there in Money? One they found in the Tallahatchie?

OSSIE. Of course I heard –

ROLLO. He heard about it, sho' nuff. Ever'body cross the south heard 'bout it.

NELLIE. And what? That kinda thang don't concern you?

OSSIE. It's not that –

ROLLO. Not that at all Nellie. It's just that these young fellas got a plan that could really do somethin'. Gonna take Natchez in a new direction. Been doin' all this – well, you tell her, Ossie.

OSSIE. Well ma'am –

ROLLO. Tell her how you been learnin' 'bout the Constitution on up there in Washington D.C. –

OSSIE. Well I've been learning about –

ROLLO. And tell her how Rev. Lee in Belzoni had came

lookin' for you to teach the old ones how to pass the tests –

OSSIE. I had written letters of support –

ROLLO. Letters to CORE. Letters to the N-A-A-C-P. Letters to get them Negro chirren in school with them Whites. My young friend here, Ossie Brown – they say he 'bout the meanest, most smartest student that D.C. done ever seen't. *(Pause.)* Go'on – tell her somethin' Ossie! What ya waitin' for?

> *(**OSSIE** looks at **ROLLO** incredulously. **NELLIE** slides forward in her chair and studies **OSSIE**.)*

OSSIE. Well...

> *(**REE ANN** enters with a tray of water.)*

REE ANN. Here ya go. Some water for you.

ROLLO. Thank you Ree Ann.

> *(She serves water to everyone. **NELLIE** accepts without batting an eye. **OSSIE** registers the servitude with discomfort, but says nothing.)*

OSSIE. *(Questionably.)* Uh...

NELLIE. Mr. Brown, you know where you is? This here ain't the north.

OSSIE. I know that, ma'am. I understand things are different down here. But different or not, there's work to do, and we've come to do it. Me and Eli, we made a pact. If one of us gets caught, the other keep going. Won't be turned around.

> *(**REE ANN** remains neutral, though she can't help but overhear. She sets the pitcher down and exits.)*

NELLIE. What you young ones feelin' ain't nothin' new.

Every Negro here in Natchez been waitin' on the winds of change. But we know how thangs work down here. We know how to keep food on our plates and keep our homes from gettin' burned to the ground. Sound to me like ya'll come down here thinkin' you know the south better than us. Tha's nothin' but northern educated arrogance.

OSSIE. With all-due respect, man can't kowtow forever.

NELLIE. What's that?

ROLLO. What he sayin', Nellie, is that sometimes you gotta push the wind in your direction a lil' if you wanna feel that breeze of change. Put a fan to it. Move the air around some. That's what my friend come to do.

NELLIE. Umhmmm... *(Beat.)* And now there's the question...why you here?

> *(**OSSIE** and **ROLLO** look at each other.)*

ROLLO. Well Nellie... I believes you already know.

> *(Beat. **NELLIE** looks at **ROLLO** squarely.)*

NELLIE. You musta done lost all ya scruples.

ROLLO. Ain't nowheres else for him to go. Every Negro I know in Natchez done already refuse him. We got to make it so he finish what he come to do.

NELLIE. Finish for what? For who? Some thangs ain't meant for Negroes to do. After what happened to that Till boy, you thank anybody with half a mind is gon' go against these White mens in Mississippi? Who gon' sign up for this? Not nobody with good sense, I tells you that.

> *(Pause. **ROLLO** looks at **NELLIE** – his shoulders broad. **OSSIE** slides forward.)*

OSSIE. We've got Brother Rollo signed up. Gonna be our first student.

(**NELLIE** *looks at* **ROLLO** *incredulously. A sobering beat.*)

NELLIE. *(To* **ROLLO.***)* When was you gon' tell me?

ROLLO. Tellin' you now.

NELLIE. When you get in yo' head to do this?

ROLLO. Been somethin' I always wanted...since long time ago. Moment never come for me – 'til right now. Got Henry Pete – gonna join in too.

NELLIE. Ol' Henry Pete? Down on Monroe? He oughta be somethin' likes seventy-years old. All kinda heart trouble he done had. Helped him with a hospital bill couple times.

ROLLO. He signin' up and we's lookin' for more.

NELLIE. Rollo, you can't do this. You tryin' to get yoself hung?

ROLLO. I'm trying to have somethin' Nellie. Somethin' what I ain't never been given befo'. When that there happened to that young Emmet, somethin' in me stopped Nellie. Way his Mama just stood up and show us all what been done to 'im. It callin' to me. She askin' for somethin'. Askin' for a difference to get made. And I wants to make that difference. For that young'un. For myself. For all of us who tired of walkin' with our heads to our feet. These fellas come down cuz they say it time to step into somethin' new. I like the sound of that. Like puttin' on a new suit, all clean lookin'. Everybody see you got to step back and take notice cuz you matter. And I'm thankin' this votin' thang...that could be a meaaaaaan suit. And I wants to wear it, Nellie. I needs you to help me get it done.

(**NELLIE** *breathes deeply.*)

NELLIE. Lawd a-mighty. *(Beat.)* What about this new Sheriff Toms? He lookin' for a reason to shut me down.

ROLLO. It's just for the week, ain't that right Ossie?

OSSIE. One week, and we go to the courthouse to register. Just teaching and training 'til then.

>(**ROLLO** *walks over to* **NELLIE**. *Grabs her hands gently.*)

ROLLO. Nellie, I always been whatever you need me to be. You know what's in these twenty years of friendship between us...all I done did at your call. Ain't mattered the kind of work it was. Just mattered it was you needin' it. And now I'm askin' you to do this for me cuz I'm needin' it. Just for once.

>(**NELLIE** *looks at* **ROLLO** – *overcome.*)

>(*A moment. A deep and contemplative breath. Finally:*)

NELLIE. I do it, Rollo. Just this once. For you.

ROLLO. That's all I'm askin'.

NELLIE. But he only gettin' a week. And I don't want none of this votin' business tracing him back here, or you gone have a mighty debt to repay.

ROLLO. We'll cover our tracks, Nellie.

>(*Long beat.*)

>(**NELLIE** *finally turns to* **OSSIE**.)

NELLIE. There's rules at this house, Mr. Brown. I 'spects you to follow 'em.

OSSIE. Certainly.

NELLIE. I gots a business. This here common room is for makin' money. Less you spendin' some, you best not be around in it.

OSSIE. Yes ma'am.

NELLIE. The gals are completely off limits. I don't 'low no Negro mens to fraternize – make me lose all my White customers...and they what keep this business goin'.

OSSIE. This brothel is segregated?

> *(Pause.* **ROLLO** *looks at* **OSSIE** *cautiously.* **NELLIE** *draws back.)*

NELLIE. You gots a problem with that?

ROLLO. He gots no problem with it at all, Nellie. No problems. Right Ossie?

> *(Moment of tension.* **OSSIE** *looks at* **ROLLO** *incredulously.)*
>
> *(***NELLIE** *eyes him deeply.* **OSSIE** *bites his tongue. Beat.)*
>
> *(Finally,* **OSSIE** *nods his head in submission.)*

NELLIE. Hmph. *(Shift.)* Dinner time's usually 'round six o'clock. I'll have my Rose come bring you a plate out to the backhouse each evenin'.

OSSIE. *(Reluctantly.)* Thank you...ma'am.

> *(***NELLIE** *moves over to the cabinet. She opens a drawer and pulls out a key.)*

NELLIE. Rollo'll show you where the backhouse is. Should already be some clean linens on the bed. You need anythang else, you go through Rollo first.

> *(***OSSIE** *looks at* **NELLIE.** *Takes the key and nods politely, in spite of himself.)*

OSSIE. Understood, madam.

ROLLO. See there, Ossie. I tol' you. Nellie Jackson be tough as nails, but got a heart of gold.

NELLIE. The work you doin', t'aint gonna go over easy. If I don't know nothin' else, I know these mens down

here. I know how they move. What they weakenesses
is. Where they rages lie. And I'm tellin' you, what you
doin' is gonna bring they hostility right to the center
of Natchez. These mens ain't gonna let you tell them
how to govern they city. They sooner see it turn to
ashes. Ya'll gonna bleed this whole town with madness
by what you tryin' to do... *(Beat.)* I keep him here for
you Rollo. It what I owe you. But Mr. Brown, you best
know what you doin'. Cuz what you startin'...ain't no
comin' back from.

(**OSSIE** *looks at* **NELLIE**. *He remains silent.)*

Go'on Rollo. Show 'im the way. He got a lotta work to
do if he tryin' to change Mississippi. Better get to it.

(**ROLLO** *heads out.* **OSSIE** *follows.* **NELLIE**
looks after them...)

Scene Three

(Lights up on **NA ROSE** *in the common room, sweeping and dusting diligently in her t-shirt and panties. It's nothing but routine for her. Comfortable and settled. She wipes sweat from her forehead. Fans herself. Removes her t-shirt, leaving her only in her bra and panties. She enjoys the cool relief and keeps sweeping.)*

(On the jukebox in mid-tune, "Getting Ready For My Daddy"* by Varetta Dillard plays. **NA ROSE** *wiggles and sways while she sweeps. The tune ends. Then in an impulse, she grabs the broom handle and it becomes her microphone.)*

NA ROSE. *(In a feigned "announcer" voice.)* Ladies and Gents, that was Varetta Dillard, "Gettin' Ready For My Daddy." But now we've got a Blues Shack favorite here tonight. Natchez, Mississippi – give a round of applause to Junior's Juke's Ravishing Rose!

*(***NA ROSE** *creates her own echo of cheering.)*

(In a whisper.) Haaaaahhh haaaaahhhhh haaaaaaaaaaaaahhhhhhhhhhhhhhhhhhh...

(She steps into her own imaginary pool of light.)

---

* A license to produce *Follow Me to Nellie's* does not include a performance license for "Getting Ready For My Daddy." The publisher and author suggest that the licensee contact ASCAP or BMI to ascertain the music publisher and contact such music publisher to license or acquire permission for performance of the song. If a license or permission is unattainable for "Getting Ready For My Daddy," the licensee may not use the song in *Follow Me to Nellie's* but should create an original composition in a similar style or use a similar song in the public domain. For further information, please see the Music and Third Party Materials Use Note on page iii.

(Feigning shyness.) Why thank you for your applause. I just loves comin' down here to this fine Blues Shack to sang for all of ya...my beloved fans. And this one here, I done wrote myself. I'ma dedicate this to you Clyde, for bein' so sweet. *(Beat.)* Awwww Miller, you jealous? Don't you worry, puddin'. I'm gon' dedicate the next song to you. *(Beat.)* Now fellas, no need to fight. There's enough of Ravishing Rose to go around!

> *(**NA ROSE** clears her throat and croons a soft tune.)*

I SIT BY THE ROSE BUSH
AND KNIT ME A DREAM
I SIT BY THE ROSE BUSH
AND KNIT ME A DREAM
'TIL I FIND ME A MAN
TO SEW UP MY SEAMS

I GOTS A HOLE IN MY HEART
THAT NEEDS SOME FILL
I GOTS A HOLE IN MY HEART
THAT NEEDS SOME FILL
COME POUR IN YOUR LOVE
BUT DOOOON'T... DON'T LET IT SPILL

I'M JUST A ROSE WITH A THORN
WILTING IN THE RAIN
AND 'TIL YOU COME AND PICK ME
I'LL BE WATER MIXED WITH PAIN

I'M JUST A ROSE WITH A THORN
WILTING IN THE RAIN
AND 'TIL YOU COME AND PICK ME
I'LL BE WATER MIXED WITH PAIN...
MIXED WITH PAIN
MIXED WITH PAAAAAAIIIIINNNNN...*

(**NA ROSE** *belts the last line out like it is her affirmation. The broom turned microphone slides down in her hands as she wails her note. When she finishes, she bows and curtsies for her fans.*)

(*Suddenly she turns as* **OSSIE BROWN** *enters from the kitchen.*)

(*Screaming.*) Oh! Oh!

OSSIE. Sorry ma'am, I –

NA ROSE. Don't look! Get back!

(**OSSIE** *turns around abruptly and covers his face.*)

(**NA ROSE** *rushes over to the couch and pulls off the throw that lay across its back. She tries to wrap herself.*)

(**OSSIE** *keeps himself turned away.*)

OSSIE. I didn't know anybody was... I thought all the girls were off...

NA ROSE. I am not one of the girls –

OSSIE. I was just hungry –

(**NA ROSE** *fidgets with tying the throw.*)

NA ROSE. You stay back! Stay turned!

OSSIE. Didn't mean no harm or no trouble. Just a guest in the backhouse and –

NA ROSE. Ainee ain't gonna like this when I tell her!

OSSIE. Ainee?

NA ROSE. I'm gon' tell her you been breakin' the rules and you gonna be gone with whatever your business is.

*(**OSSIE** turns to speak.)*

Don't look, I say!

*(**OSSIE** turns back around sharply.)*

OSSIE. Sorry, miss. You just...you got me wrong now –

NA ROSE. I don't gots you nothin'! You ain't supposin' to be in the house. That's what I know. Ainee told me. I know what the rules is.

OSSIE. I was just hungry –

NA ROSE. Hmph! Not supposin' to be in the house...

*(**OSSIE** tries to turn his head slowly.)*

OSSIE. You decent yet, ma'am?

NA ROSE. I'm always decent!

OSSIE. I'm just meaning... Can I turn around now please?

NA ROSE. Just you hold it! *(She fidgets with the throw.)* Ugh! This thang!

> *(**NA ROSE** finalizes her fixings with the throw. She wears it like a long gown. She looks awkward. Weird. Her skinny arms stick out like twigs. It slides and she keeps her hands on it to hold it up.)*

> *(**OSSIE** doesn't wait for permission. He turns around to view her for the first time fully. He finds her awkwardness charming. A wide smile spreads across his face.)*

Nothin' but rudeness.

OSSIE. *(Softens his smile.)* My apologies ma'am. Like I was telling you, I didn't know anybody was home.

NA ROSE. Ainee say you out in the backhouse only or you out of a place to stay.

(**OSSIE** *looks at her peculiarly.*)

OSSIE. Ainee?

NA ROSE. That'd be Miss Nellie Jackson to you!

OSSIE. Oh yes, indeed. The Madam. My apologies. I was just a little hungry. A gentleman needs his morning fuel to get him going. That's all. No trouble.

NA ROSE. I was fixin' to bring it up in a moment. Sit it out there on the back stairs for you like every morn.

OSSIE. Today was just a little later than usual so I –

NA ROSE. Well!

OSSIE. So I just figured nobody was home. Thought maybe folks were too busy to remember me today.

NA ROSE. (*Mumbling.*) Had a lot of cleanin'.

OSSIE. Well that I can see. And a fine cleaning job you do there. Place has an extra touch of sparkle and shine cuz of you. I can see that real well.

(**NA ROSE** *softens a touch.*)

NA ROSE. Made grits and eggs this mornin'. I can go warm 'em on the stove for you now.

OSSIE. No need miss. I helped myself already. They were mighty tasty, those grits and eggs. You put your foot in 'em.

NA ROSE. Well... (*Flattered.*) ...just grits and eggs...

(*Beat.* **NA ROSE** *stands awkwardly still.*)

(**OSSIE** *smiles again. It is warm and enticing.* **NA ROSE** *is befuddled...with this moment... mostly with herself...*)

OSSIE. You sing pretty.

NA ROSE. (*Embarrassed.*) Oh! You spy!

OSSIE. Oh no, no...

NA ROSE. Rudeness!

OSSIE. I just... I couldn't help hearing...

NA ROSE. Ain't supposed to be in the house anyways!

OSSIE. Your voice just got me stuck. Didn't want to leave really. Sound was too pretty.

NA ROSE. Pretty?

OSSIE. Oh yes, miss... *(Beat.)* It *is* miss?

> *(**NA ROSE** nods impatiently.)*

Yes, pretty indeed. Sounded like a tune at the Blues Shack, but better. Your voice just got a real sweet and soft kinda harmony to it. Make a man stop in his tracks... *(Beat.)* I'm sorry for...listening...

NA ROSE. Well I 'spose...if you couldn't help yaself... *(Beat.)* Sound like somethin' at the Blues Shack, you say?

OSSIE. Indeed. Better. You made that one up, did you?

NA ROSE. And how you knowin' this?

OSSIE. Never heard it before. I listen to my bit of the blues, miss. Never heard those lyrics you were singing though.

NA ROSE. They my own.

OSSIE. Your own? Well...you've got a special kind of talent.

> *(Pause. A moment of attraction. **OSSIE** eyes the jukebox.)*

I didn't know that thing worked.

NA ROSE. Well...really it ain't 'spose to be...on right now...

OSSIE. It's a real beauty.

NA ROSE. Plays real good too.

OSSIE. I wasn't talkin' 'bout the jukebox.

>   *(Beat.)*

NA ROSE. What your name be?

OSSIE. What's yours?

NA ROSE. Name Na Rose.

OSSIE. Pleasure to meet you, Na Rose. I'm Ossie Brown.

>   *(**NA ROSE** gasps. Taking in the full danger
>   and intrigue of **OSSIE**.)*

No worries miss. I'm not half as bad as you probably heard.

NA ROSE. You that...one what's runnin' from the law?

OSSIE. Listen I... I'd sure appreciate it if you wouldn't...if you could keep this encounter between us. I'd be in a heap of trouble if...well...you understand?

>   *(**NA ROSE** nods, still gazing at **OSSIE** in awe.)*

Thank you kindly, miss.

NA ROSE. And I'd 'preciate it if you –

OSSIE. Oh don't you worry. Nobody'll hear a peep out of me about any of this. Your blues is safe with me... *(Beat / he winks.)* Ravishing Rose.

NA ROSE. *(Smiling.)* Oh...

>   *(**OSSIE** laughs. **NA ROSE** turns pink – no
>   matter her complexion.)*

>   *(A sound of a back door closing from the
>   kitchen. **NA ROSE** and **OSSIE** look startled.)*

SANDY. *(Offstage.)* Marla! Told you them thangs don't match!

MARLA. *(Offstage.)* Shoot! Did I 'member to turn off that hose out front?

NA ROSE. *(To* **OSSIE**.*)* Oh! You best git!

REE ANN. *(Offstage.)* I'll go check.

> (**NA ROSE** *shoos* **OSSIE** *toward the door.)*

(Offstage.) It's turned off!

> (**NA ROSE** *opens the door.* **OSSIE** *hurls out and crashes right into* **REE ANN** *as she enters. The shopping bags in her arms fall to the floor, sending ladies undies and lingerie flying across the yard.)*

Owwww!

OSSIE. Oh! Sorry there ma'am!

REE ANN. I'll be damned.

> (**REE ANN** *rubs her arm.)*

OSSIE. You alright?

REE ANN. Just barely. Thangs all over the place...

OSSIE. My mistake, let me help you...

> (**REE ANN** *goes to pick up the bras and panties displayed all over the yard.* **OSSIE** *attempts to help. Touches the panties as if they are toxic.* **NA ROSE** *snatches the panties from him and hands them to* **REE ANN**.*)*

NA ROSE. Here ya go Ree Ann.

REE ANN. Thank you Na Rose.

> (*For the first time,* **REE ANN** *looks at* **NA ROSE** *fully. Sees the scene before her.* **NA ROSE** *in the throw.* **OSSIE** *and* **NA ROSE**. *Together.)*

> *(Beat. Beat. Beat.)*

(**SANDY** *and* **MARLA** *enter from the kitchen into the common room with their shopping bags.*)

SANDY. Nellie told you 'bout matchin' 'em.

MARLA. Damn thangs cost too much by the pair. I gots me five for the price of one panties and five for the price of one brassieres. And they gon' go together whether they likes it or not!

SANDY. I'm gettin' Ree Ann. She'll tell it true.

(**SANDY** *runs over to the side door.*)

(*Stops when she sees the three in the yard.*)

Oh! Sorry...

REE ANN. I recognize this fella. Come here with Rollo the other day. Must be our secret guest from the backhouse. That right?

OSSIE.	**SANDY.**
And I was just heading back there now.	(*Whispering to* **MARLA.***)* Oh! The secret guest!
REE ANN.	**MARLA.**
What was you doin' down here in the first place?	Where he at?

(**MARLA** *rushes to* **SANDY**'s *side and peeks out the door.*)

NA ROSE. Hungry he say. And I was just tellin' him that I was gonna put his food out for him real quick in a hurry.

REE ANN. Nellie made the rules real clear. She catch you 'round here Mr...

OSSIE. – Brown. –

REE ANN. Mr. Brown, she's liable to throw you right out.

OSSIE. I understand ma'am and I promise it won't happen again –

MARLA. Awww who cares 'bout Nellie? He hungry? Let 'im eat!

> (**MARLA** *pushes out of the door and walks over to* **OSSIE**.*)*

Name's Marla.

OSSIE. Hello ma'am.

SANDY. *(From the doorway – eagerly.)* I'm Sandy!

MARLA. Why don't you come on inside and tell us what bring you to Natchez whilst we fix you up somethin'.

NA ROSE. I made some grits and eggs –

MARLA. Some real food for you.

> (**NA ROSE** *scowls at* **MARLA**.*)*

OSSIE. No thank you, ma'am. I'm good and stuffed now. Grits and eggs did me just the way I like.

> *(He eyes* **NA ROSE**. *She blushes.)*

MARLA. Well come let us show you our new jukebox. You like the blues?

REE ANN. Marla he ain't got time to fraternize! He best be gettin' back to his room.

OSSIE. That's right. I really have a lot of work to do, so sorry to intrude. If you'll excuse me. *(He slides past them all.)* Good day to you ladies.

> (**OSSIE** *takes one final look at* **NA ROSE** *again before heading off.)*

> *(The women watch him leave and salivate over him.)*

SANDY. Oooo weee!!!!! Ain't he delicious?!

MARLA. Finer than Jim.

REE ANN. Had no business bein' out here like that. None at all. Put all us in harm's way. He ought to know better... work he come to do. People talk.

NA ROSE. What people?

SANDY. What work?

> (**REE ANN** *eyes* **NA ROSE** *in the throw for a moment. She fixes her lips to question, but decides against it.*)

REE ANN. Best get in the house now. All of you.

MARLA. *(To* **NA ROSE.***)* Nice dress.

> (**NA ROSE** *scowls at* **MARLA** *again... The women take* **REE ANN***'s lead into the house.)*

REE ANN. That fella, he be trouble. Nellie kick him out fa sho' if she knew he was makin' busy with the rest of us.

MARLA. Well ain't nobody gonna tell her. No snitches 'round here. Right Na Rose?

SANDY. Why he be trouble?

REE ANN. Never you mind, Sandy. Just make sho' you ain't talkin' 'bout seein' him here. None of you.

SANDY. He dangerous?

MARLA. Hot damn! He that fella, ain't he?

REE ANN. Marla hush yo' trap!

SANDY. What fella?

MARLA. One what runnnin' from the law! Gots a bit of unusual to him.

REE ANN. Marla gotdamm! I say shush!

SANDY. That be that Ossie Brown?

MARLA. Ain't that 'bout nothin'? Miss Nellie Jackson's Whorehouse harboring votin' mens.

REE ANN. He ain't supposed to be in the house. Supposed to stay out in that backhouse so nobody catch him here. Negro man settlin' in here gon' raise more than a few eyebrows, 'less he runnin' errands.

NA ROSE. What'll happen if he gets caught?

REE ANN. You don't wanna begin that story. Don't end in no kinda pretty.

MARLA. I knew it was somethin' extra sexy 'bout that man. Got him a sizzle to him. Bet he haughty. Walk with his shoulders pulled back. Somethin' in him got a different kinda presence.

SANDY. Didn't know he'd be so handsome!

NA ROSE. *(Almost to herself.)* And he got a special way of talkin' to you...

> *(**NA ROSE** is taken. **REE ANN** catches this. Looks at her cautiously.)*

REE ANN. That's enough of that. Ain't sayin' one more thing about it. And neither is none of you. Keep it locked and sealed. Ya'll hear?

SANDY. Not a peep.

MARLA. Scouts honor.

REE ANN. Good. Now go'on in the kitchen and I'll cook you up some chicken and biscuits.

MARLA. Now THAT'S a meal!

> *(**MARLA** and **SANDY** trail off into the kitchen. **REE ANN** falls back with **NA ROSE**.)*

REE ANN. Best go change into somethin' now.

NA ROSE. I was...just fixin' to...

REE ANN. And it may be...best to stay from near that backhouse...no matter what kinda way he talk to you. Catch me?

> (**NA ROSE** *nods.*)

NA ROSE. Caught ya.

REE ANN. Good. Now go'on put on some clothes...'fore folks start thankin' you one of us.

> (**NA ROSE** *nods and heads to her room.* **REE ANN** *watches after her with concern.*)

MARLA. *(Offstage.)* Ree Ann! Let's get to them chicken and biscuits you promised!

REE ANN. I'm comin', Marl. *(Beat.)* I'm comin...

> (**REE ANN** *sighs, shakes her head, and takes off to the kitchen.*)

Scene Four

(Lights up on the bedroom of **NELLIE JACKSON**. *She sits in her nightgown at her boudoir.* **NA ROSE** *brushes* **NELLIE***'s hair.* **NELLIE** *rocks to the rhythm of* **NA ROSE***'s song.)*

NA ROSE.

I GOT BLUES IN MY CUPBOARDS
BLUES ON MY SHELF
BLUES IN THE CLOSET
NOW LEAVE ME TO MYSELF...*

> *(***NELLIE** *smiles as* **NA ROSE** *hums along. Suddenly,* **NELLIE** *has a coughing spasm.* **NA ROSE** *stops humming and tends to her.)*

You alright, Ainee?

NELLIE. *(Composing herself.)* I'm fine sugar. Your voice is like medicine, it is Rose. Softens the ails.

NA ROSE. I loves sangin', I do.

NELLIE. You ought to. It's your way of giving somethin'. *(Beat.)* You check the jar tonight?

NA ROSE. Yes Ainee. It's all in. Everybody turned in their share. *(An afterthought.)* Even Marla.

NELLIE. Did she now? *(Pensive / beat.)* Thank you Rose, darlin'. It's real good I got you around with yo' young eyes. That Marla'll try to get anything over on me she can.

> *(Beat.* **NA ROSE** *continues brushing* **NELLIE***'s*

---

* A license to produce *Follow Me to Nellie's* does not include a performance license for any third-party or copyrighted music. Licensees should create an original melody. For further information, please see the Music and Third Party Materials Use Note on page iii.

hair.)

That should be good. Thanks for brushing, honey. My hands just been a lil' stiff lately. Hard to brush it myself...and Lord knows I can't have no unkempt head of hair.

NA ROSE. One braid or two?

NELLIE. Just one a be fine.

> (**NA ROSE** *begins to put* **NELLIE**'s *hair into one plait.)*

Thinkin' you and Rollo gon' need to take a trip for me. Down to Louisiana. Need you to carry some Bourbon over for me.

NA ROSE. You want me bootleg?

NELLIE. Ain't nothin' but ridin' sweet and pretty and pretendin' like you a call girl. And you wear you a big enough skirt so's you can sit on top of them cases and cover 'em good. We'll show ya just how it's done.

NA ROSE. I thought you swore off bootleggin' from that time the police almost caught you.

NELLIE. Well, I did. Promised to God if he got me outta that situation, I wasn't never gonna ride no whiskey in from Louisiana no more. If I wasn't ridin' with White mens, them patrolmen woulda grabbed me fa sho'. I'da been under the jail by now. But I'm gon' have to pick back up the business some. This new Sheriff Toms... he gon' require some special tricks. Got to make him good and happy with the way of things so he leave 'em be. 'Sides...this here ain't whiskey, is it? And I'm not the one ridin' it, now am I?

NA ROSE. *(Laughing softly.)* Oh Ainee...

NELLIE. Me and God do a lot of negotiating. Got to. Only way for a Negro woman to make her own way here is to break the rules a little. You ain't had to learn that yet, and I pray you won't never have to. But that be the way of it. *(Beat.)* You left that dinner plate on the back staircase like I toldja, right?

NA ROSE. Yes Ainee. Gave that Mr. Brown the biggest pork chop of us all.

>*(Pause.* **NELLIE** *turns to* **NA ROSE**.*)*

NELLIE. How you know his name?

>*(***NA ROSE*** *stiffens.)*

NA ROSE. I... I believe you callin' him that once...

NELLIE. *(Unmoved.)* That what you believe.

NA ROSE. Yes, Ainee...

NELLIE. Hmmm...

>*(Beat.)*

Grab my sleep cap in my drawer for me.

>*(***NA ROSE*** *goes over to the drawer and pulls out the parchment from her pocket, studying it in her hands.* **NELLIE** *doesn't watch her. She remains contemplative.)*

>*(***NA ROSE*** *pulls out a sleeping cap. In one hand, the cap. In the other, the parchment.)*

NA ROSE. *(Softly.)* Ainee...there's somethin' I wanna talk to you about –

NELLIE. You know, this cough still ain't right.

>*(***NA ROSE*** *folds the parchment and puts it back in her pocket. She puts the cap on* **NELLIE**.*)*

NA ROSE. What ya mean, Ainee?

NELLIE. Been to the Doctor. Down to the pharmacy. Don't

nobody know what to call it. Just say it's a cough won't go away...

NA ROSE. It'll be alright, won't it?

NELLIE. I ain't so sho'...

> (**NELLIE** *grabs* **NA ROSE***'s hand sits her on the bed gently. Motherly.*)

I done drawed up a will, just in case.

NA ROSE. In case what?

NELLIE. In case it don't get alright.

NA ROSE. Ainee, don't talk that way.

NELLIE. I got to. Now I don't wants none of the others hearin' 'bout this to get them to frettin'. But I'm tellin' you, Rose, cuz I want you to know... I'm leavin' this house to you when I'm gone.

NA ROSE. Oh Ainee... I don't know if I could...

NELLIE. I done made my mind up.

NA ROSE. But Ainee, this yo' house. I wouldn't know what to –

NELLIE. I'm not sayin' you have to keep it the kind of place it is now. Best not stay this way forever. This here been all I done ever known't. This face and skin done cost me a lot, but when I wasn't nothin' but a girl of yo' age, this here what I found to be good at. Knowin' mens... how to lay with 'em. Done had it took from me more times than I care to remember. But I learned what to do with it. How to make it somethin' what can earn my livin'. Woman on her lonesome either take or get took. And I done figured out how to get me some land with it. How to get me a house bought and put in my name. How to have somethin' to stand on. *(Beat.)* I got a lot to answer for to God, but one thang I know is this here hookin' ain't for you.

NA ROSE. But Ainee, what if I...if I don't stay around here? What'll happen if I leave or –

NELLIE. Oh Rose, don't leave. Say you won't. Say you'll keep this land I done worked so hard for. Be the one I can leave somethin' to.

NA ROSE. I wants to sing, Ainee. Gots a blues band comin' after me. Sayin' they take me around with 'em and tour the south. Maybe I can be somethin' that way.

NELLIE. You want to leave?

NA ROSE. I just...

NELLIE. Life of a blueswoman ain't for you, Rose. It don't lead to nothin' much better than what I been through. Women singin' them tunes only get that way through lots heartache and despair. Can't sing the blues without it.

NA ROSE. But Ainee, I love it. It's what I wants to do.

NELLIE. I'm tryin' to give you somethin' better than that, Rose. I done always known that's what I was here to do. You remember me finding you when you was a little one?

NA ROSE. Of course Ainee. I always remember.

NELLIE. Rollo come to me. Middle of that nasty hurricane, bangin' on my door cuz he seen you lyin' there, storm-tossed. Sleepin' on that scrap piece of cardboard. Motherless. And I knowed it right then I was supposed to be somethin' to you. Give you shelter and love. *(Beat.)* I know Negroes ain't got nothin' to stand on if it ain't land. I want you to have this and make it somethin' better. Find you a husband. You pretty as the sun. Everybody gonna want some of your rays... So you finds you the best one and marry him. Have some chirren. Keep the house and make it be for family.

NA ROSE. But Ainee...

NELLIE. You my daughter. The onliest one I done ever known. You all I got to give to anything to. I'm passin' you this land for legacy. Keep it for me, Rose. Give me ease 'fore I goes off to sleep in case I don't wake back up.

(**NA ROSE** *inhales a long breath.*)

NA ROSE. Get you some rest, Ainee. It'll be alright. Just need to get some rest.

(*She takes* **NELLIE**'s *hand and kisses it.*)

(*Then she takes the parchment from her pocket, toils with it for a moment, and crumples it.*)

'Nite Ainee.

(*Lights shift.*)

Scene Five

(Lights up on the common room. NELLIE preps the space for company. She is adorned in baseball paraphernalia.)

(ROLLO enters in a ballcap, finishing a hotdog.)

NELLIE. Gals oughta be gettin' ready. Told the boys to come by here 'round seven o'clock. After a winning game, they gonna be good and ready to celebrate.

ROLLO. The boys was lit up tonight. You see the way Jameson slid into third? Ain't never seen him run like that in his whole time on the Indians.

NELLIE. Think this talk goin' around about a new stadium put a little pepper in 'em?

ROLLO. Maybe so.

NELLIE. How thangs lookin'? Sound like Sheriff Toms gonna take us up on our proposal?

ROLLO. Well likes I toldja, he sendin' his son over this evenin' to have a lil' talk about it. I think we stands a good chance of gettin' on his good side if we welcome him right.

NELLIE. I'll make sho' of it. *(Shift.)* Open the cabinet and pull out a bag of nickels. Need to fill this place with some sounds.

(ROLLO moves over to the cabinet, takes out his key, and unlocks it.)

(He pulls out a giant plastic bag filled with nickel rolls.)

ROLLO. Na Rose best be comin' along soon so we can get rollin' over to Louisiana and back 'fore the sun come up.

NELLIE. I'll call her down.

> (**NELLIE** *exits toward the rooms.* **ROLLO** *counts out the nickels.*)

(Offstage.) Rose! Come on down so you and Rollo be goin' off soon! And gals, be gettin' ready! Put on those new drawers I gave ya'll money for!

> (**NELLIE** *coughs harshly. She stops and checks to see if* **ROLLO** *notices. Oblivious, he counts nickels.*)

ROLLO. How many bags?

NELLIE. Just half a dollar's worth. We get the fellas all warmed up and enjoyin' the good music so they be inclined to pull out they own nickels to keep it goin'.

ROLLO. Right. *(Shift.)* We gotta get Sheriff Tom's boy to talk to us right 'bout Eli Perkins too. Get his bail posted. Family gettin' worried. And what's bad for Eli be bad for Ossie too.

NELLIE. His mama stay ringin' me. Even sent over one of his auntie's in the next county to come askin' me for some influence. Don't know what these folks thankin' I can do.

ROLLO. Thankin' you can help, is all. You the only Negro woman they know got the ear of the law and the money to make anythang happen over here. They got good reason to worry. Say them Vernon Boys been showin' up 'round that jailhouse after hours. Sheriff Tom's been keepin' 'em at bay.

NELLIE. Vernon Boys? That ain't no kinda good. *(Beat.)* Has they come messin' with you too? Down at that schoolhouse?

ROLLO. No, we ain't had no troubles. Been real private. Just been learnin' how to interpret thangs on that Constitution to pass them tests. Hear tell when they did it in Belzoni, them crackers was askin' all kinds of crazy questions to keep Negroes from passin'. "How many bubbles in a bar of soap?" Ossie say.

NELLIE. That one of the questions they ask?

ROLLO. Thas what Ossie say.

NELLIE. Well who can answer that? Is that what them White folks do when they wash? Count bubbles? No wonders they runnin' everythang. Ain't not a Negro in this world got that kinda time on they hands to be doin' some damn bubble countin'.

ROLLO. Ossie say they want us to give up. Get us frustrated so we backs off.

NELLIE. *(Faintly.)* Well, maybe you oughta.

> *(***ROLLO*** looks at ***NELLIE*** – hurt.)*

ROLLO. Nellie.

NELLIE. I just... I...wonders if you ain't maybe just a lil' ahead yourself, here.

ROLLO. You thankin' I can't make my own mind up as man? That what you thankin' of me?

NELLIE. I ain't say that. I just...

> *(Pause. ***NELLIE*** looks at ***ROLLO***. Love and concern. They stare at each other silently.)*

> *(A young white man, ***TOM JR.***, enters into the yard and knocks on the side door.)*

Oh – that must be him. Quick, put on that Lil' Walter.

> *(***ROLLO*** goes to the jukebox and inserts a nickel. ***NELLIE*** removes her baseball gear, pulls a fancy housecoat from a coat rack, and slips it on.)*

(Little Walter's "Juke" plays from the jukebox. The knocking at the door persists. **NELLIE** goes to answer.)*

(Feigning surprised.) Well hello there sir. What can I do you for this fine evenin'?

TOM JR. *(Removing his hat.)* Here to see Miss Nellie Jackson, ma'am. Saw the red and white awnin' – figure this must be the house they tole me 'bout.

NELLIE. And you must be the son of Sheriff Thomas Robertson. That so?

TOM JR. That's correct ma'am. Name's Tom Jr.

NELLIE. Well please come on in, Mr. Tom Jr. I'm Miss Nellie.

> *(**NELLIE** motions for him to enter. He takes a very curious look around; mesmerized.)*

TOM JR. Lively place you got here, ma'am.

NELLIE. Yes. We keep it full of spirits. Rollo, get Mr. Tom Jr. a glass of brandy from our top shelf.

ROLLO. 'Course.

TOM JR. Well thank you ma'am. I do appreciate it.

> *(**ROLLO** goes over to the cabinet and pours **TOM** a drink.)*

NELLIE. Mr. Tom, I've been talkin' to your paw. Good fella,

---

he is. I'm sho' you know him an' me gots some thangs we need sortin' out.

TOM JR. Well, yes ma'am. That's why he sendin' me along. I'm his new deputy. And I wants to make a nice presence with the people of Natchez. Warm and friendly like, y'know? Lookin' to get along real fine together, us folks.

NELLIE. Well that sounds real good, Mr. Tom. I believe in the same thang.

TOM JR. I wanna see to it that Negroes get a fair shake here in Natchez. I'm a real believer in it too. Even believe in what they did with them kids and that school integratin'. Paw ain't too happy 'bout that, but I thank he just needs a lil' mo' time than me. I thank it's only fair folks get a chance to have good education and all that. I'm on the Negro side. You can bet it.

NELLIE. I see there. Well, we are happy to have you on our side Mr. Tom.

TOM JR. Only thang is, with Pop just takin' office an' all, we got to make some of these changes happen slow. Ya understand?

NELLIE. Well sho'.

TOM JR. So Pop just wants to make sho' that this talk goin' 'round 'bout these outside agitators comin' here to rile up the Negroes 'gainst the courts...that ya'll keep yaselves free from it. We got that Eli Perkins in jail, but ain't no tellin' where his partner done run off to. We lookin' for him. I ain't 'gainst what they tryin' to do personally, but it's just bringin' a whole lotta upset to others around us. Lord knows Pop don't wanna upset folks when he just gettin' foot in Natchez good.

> (*Pause.* **ROLLO** *looks at* **NELLIE,** *but they both remain calm.*)

NELLIE. You ain't got to worry 'bout us with no votin'

business. We only got one kinda rule we break around here, Mr. Tom. But there's a concern about that we need to discuss.

TOM JR. I thank I understand where this is headin' ma'am. And I been sent to tell you that your proposal to help with the new stadium is lookin' real good to Pop.

NELLIE. Lookin' good enough to settle my books?

TOM JR. Well, so long as you keep the money circulating in a particular way, Pop agrees to leave you to your own vices.

NELLIE. And what way is that Mr. Tom?

TOM JR. Outta legal affairs ma'am. So long as you just operatin' this...fine establishment, and that's all, you won't have no troubles from Pop.

NELLIE. Legal affairs... I see...

ROLLO. Well suh, what about that little matter with Eli –

NELLIE. We understands what you meanin' Mr. Tom. Understand real good.

> (**NELLIE** *looks at* **ROLLO**. *He hesistates for a moment, and backs off.*)

> (**TOM JR**. *eyes the jukebox. He approaches it.*)

TOM JR. This is some kinda jukebox you got! Never seen one inside a house before. Not never.

NELLIE. Got it special delivered. Any blues song you wanna hear, you just tells me and we'll play it for you. You like the blues?

TOM JR. Love it. Used to listen to it all the time in the Delta. Go over to Nawlins (*"New Orleans."*) or at the Blues Shack here in Natchez. Seen Howlin' Wolf hisself one time, I did.

NELLIE. Well, anytime you don't wanna spend all your

dimes down at the Blues Shack just to hear some blues, you come right here and we'll take care of you. If'n you wants anythang else this evenin', we can take care of that too.

TOM JR. Well, I...

> (**NELLIE** *goes over to the side of the room and leans offstage.*)

NELLIE. *(Yelling.)* Sandy! Come on down here! Got ourselves a special client!

TOM JR. Oh no, ma'am. I was just stoppin' by to introduce myself. Makin' rounds. Don't mean to patronize –

> (**NA ROSE** *enters all dressed up.*)

NA ROSE. Sorry to take so long. Was lookin' for my shawl. I'm ready now.

> (**TOM JR.** *stares at* **NA ROSE** *hungrily. He is captivated by her beauty.*)

TOM JR. Well... I really wasn't gonna indulge ma'am but... *(Beat / stares at* **NA ROSE.***)* she sho' is purrrrty.

> (**NELLIE** *scoops* **NA ROSE** *off to the side.*)

NELLIE. Not her, Mr. Tom. She's runnin' out now with Rollo. But I've got one of my special gals for you. High yella and plump and firm. *(Leans offstage.)* Sandy!

> (**TOM JR.***'s eyes stay fixed on* **NA ROSE.** *He studies her intensely.*)

TOM JR. *(To* **NA ROSE.***)* Forgive me starin'. But, haven't I seen you somewhere before, miss?

> (**NA ROSE** *is taken aback. Startled.*)

NA ROSE. Me? Nah...sir...

TOM JR. You sure? I never forget a face...'specially one as purrty as yours.

(**SANDY** *enters looking all dolled up. She wears high heels, stockings, a beautiful lace negligee, and a silk robe.*)

NELLIE. There you are, Sandy. This here's Mr. Tom Jr., Sheriff Tom's son. Go'on do him good. Give him the best treatment you got.

SANDY. Sure thang. (*To* **TOM JR**.) Hey there honey, come wit' Sandy. She'll make it taste so sweet you'd thank it was made of sugar...

TOM JR. (*Uncertainly.*) Well...that sounds nice...but I um...

(**SANDY** *drags* **TOM JR**. *off toward the bedroom. He stops to give another inquisitive glance back to* **NA ROSE**.)

(**SANDY** *takes her finger to his chin and turns his head in her direction.*)

SANDY. Come on, darlin'. I gots somethin' good saved just for you.

(*She tries to lead* **TOM JR**. *off to the bedroom. He follows for a helpless moment, and then pulls away.*)

TOM JR. No, no, thank you for the compliments, Miss Jackson, but I must be goin'. Got to finish makin' my rounds.

SANDY. I'll be back there waitin' if you change ya mind.

(**SANDY** *blows him a kiss and exits.* **TOM JR**. *looks weak enough to crumble. He turns to* **NELLIE**.)

TOM JR. But you be sure to pass the word to your folks... about...that runaway agitator. Vernon Boys are lookin' for 'em now that the word's out. And well...we wants to make sho' everybody's alright.

NELLIE. Surely, Mr. Tom. Will do.

> (**TOM JR**. *tips his hat and exits.*)
>
> (**NELLIE** *closes the door and looks sternly at* **ROLLO**.)

You heard alla that good?

ROLLO. *(Firmly.)* I ain't changin' my mind. *(Beat.)* Why you cut me off 'bout Eli's bail? Was the perfect time to talk to him.

NELLIE. My books lookin' good, he say. I can't double back and mess that up again.

ROLLO. But you heard it Nellie. Them Vernon Boys –

NELLIE. I already gots me a lot on the line, Rollo. For you and that Mr. Brown. And I can't lose this house. That one thang I can't do. Now ya'll gon' have to get Eli's bail from someplace else. I can't be everythang for every-Negro-body in this county. This time folks is gonna have to do it without Nellie Jackson.

> *(Beat.)*

ROLLO. Well then, I guess we gonna.

NELLIE. Ya'll best git onto Vidalia and get the liquor 'fore that sun catch you.

> (**ROLLO** *stares at* **NELLIE** *defiantly. Then he puts on his hat and turns away.*)

ROLLO. You know Nellie...if I ain't know no better... I'd thank you just as against us as these crackers. And I really hopin' that ain't so.

NELLIE. Rollo...

ROLLO. Come on, Lil' Bit. Let's go'on.

> (**NELLIE** *fumes silently.*)

(**NA ROSE** *follows* **ROLLO** *into the yard. The sound of a truck pulling away.*)

(**NELLIE** *fluffs a pillow. Puts another nickel in the jukebox. Muddy Waters, "Hoochie Coochie Man,"* plays.*)

(*The sound of another truck pulling up. Headlights beam from outside.*)

(**NELLIE** *runs over to the side door and peers out. The grandfather clock chimes.*)

NELLIE. Seven o'clock gals! The boys are here!

(**NELLIE** *coughs furiously and tries to compose herself.*)

Let's get to it!

(*Lights shift.*)

---

* A license to produce *Follow Me to Nellie's* does not include a performance license for "Hoochie Coochie Man." The publisher and author suggest that the licensee contact ASCAP or BMI to ascertain the music publisher and contact such music publisher to license or acquire permission for performance of the song. If a license or permission is unattainable for "Hoochie Coochie Man," the licensee may not use the song in *Follow Me to Nellie's* but should create an original composition in a similar style or use a similar song in the public domain. For further information, please see the Music and Third Party Materials Use Note on page iii.

Scene Six

(Lights up on the gals' room. **REE ANN** *and* **MARLA** *getting ready for bed.)*

MARLA. Sandy still at it?

REE ANN. Should be on her last. She done had a full night and I hopin' she done soon. I'm good and tired. Next time, you know who to go to for board.

MARLA. Well goodie for her. She can take mine if it please her. I ain't too keen on these ballplayers. And that one, tall one with the red hair, he nearly make me wanna grab him by his sausage and eggs and pinch 'em right off him, way he talkin' to me.

REE ANN. Marla you get too fiery 'bout it all. Better be easy some. Just work.

MARLA. How you say it that way – just work? Don't you get a lil' tired sometimes? Wanna be talked to different?

REE ANN. I want a lotta thangs. Don't mean they gon' come. Best not to be pinin' your hopes on nothin' imaginary.

MARLA. Still don't mean they got to say all the things they do. Ain't 'spose to talk street to you up in here. Might as well be at the riverboat.

REE ANN. Somebody said somethin' to you ain't right, you just got to tell Nellie. She don't 'low for nothin' indecent. What they say?

MARLA. Never you mind. Forgets I said anything at all. *(Shift.)* I gots somethin' I wants you to read for me.

REE ANN. Somethin' like what?

MARLA. Telegram. From Jim. Been keepin' it. 'Fraid of what it might say.

*(**MARLA** pulls a telegram from her pillowcase.*

Hands it to **REE ANN**.)

Read it for me. Please.

> *(Unenthusiastically,* **REE ANN** *reads the note. Stops. A bit of surprise.)*

What it be? Somethin' bad? He alright?

REE ANN. He say...they found somethin' in his leg. Some kinda material. Been discharged.

MARLA. Has he?!? That mean he comin' for me?!

REE ANN. Say...he comin' home.

MARLA. You ain't kiddin'?!

> *(***MARLA*** snatches the letter and tries to read for herself. Points at the bottom of it.)*

What's that sayin' right there?

REE ANN. *(Slightly hesitant.)* Say love. Love, Jim.

MARLA. Love Jim! *(Smiling brightly.)* Hot damn, he comin' for me! I tol' you so! Ain't that somethin'? I can't believes it!

REE ANN. It's somethin'.

> *(***MARLA*** looks at **REE ANN**, who tucks herself into bed. Less than enthusiastic.)*

> *(Pause.* **MARLA** *holds the telegram in her hands, smiling for a moment. Enjoying its feeling. Then she looks over to* **REE ANN**. *Approaches her bedside.)*

MARLA. You know, Ree Ann...sometimes it ain't bad to pine for somethin'. I rather have somethin' to hope for than nothin' at all. I thankin' so since that Mr. Brown done come around. He bringin' change with him, and I can feels it. Thought thangs wun'nt ever gon' be no better than what they is, but now...maybe so...and that be a good thang, Ree Ann. That be a real good thang.

REE ANN. 'Nite Marl.

MARLA. 'Nite Ree Ann.

> *(Lights crossfade to the yard.)*
>
> *(**TOM JR**. walks up and looks around the house.)*
>
> *(**OSSIE** walks into the yard casually, and suddenly sees **TOM**. They both halt and look at each other.)*

TOM JR. Lookin' for somethin', friend?

OSSIE. *(Faking southern.)* Oh, uh...no...naw suh. Just... just takin' a short cut home. Cut through this yard sometimes cuz it's faster...

TOM JR. Not a late-night patron?

OSSIE. Me? Oh naw, sir. Hear tell this place don't even 'low no Colored mens inside.

TOM JR. Oh yep. That's right, all right. *(Beat.)* 'Tween you an' me, there's one of 'em in there I'd sho' like to see again. But seems she ain't for sale no way.

> *(**OSSIE**'s brow raises.)*

OSSIE. That right sir?

TOM JR. Pretty thang, she is. Was just makin' my rounds like I do some nights. Thought maybe I could catch her. Seen her comin' in 'round this hour before. *(Beat.)* Where you live, fella?

OSSIE. On up the road there. Few blocks north.

TOM JR. On Pearl Street?

OSSIE. Yessir. Exactly.

TOM JR. Cuttin' through this yard is private property, y'know?

OSSIE. Yessir. Just tryin' to get home as fast as I can. Long day, sir.

TOM JR. Well that's a good idea. You wanna get home quick at this hour. Climate's real bad since those northern fellas come down and done got folks angry. Vernon Boys lookin' for 'em.

OSSIE. Yessir, I mighta heard that.

TOM JR. Yes, well... I don't wants nothin' to get out of hand. *(Beat / twinge of sadness.)* Done seen thangs outta hand before. Saw a man once – 'cused of stealin' pears from the family grocery over in Biloxi. Belonged to my uncles. They used to look after me. Bring me 'long with 'em sometime. I seen when they caught that man. Stripped his shirt off 'im. Took a whole bucket of hot tar and poured it on his bare skin. Seem like he was meltin' right in front of me. Then they take a case of feathers from the stuffin' of a pillow. Poured the feathers to that man 'til he looked like some kinda freak. Took me a long time 'fore I sleep at night without gettin' this hauntin' feelin' in my gut.

> *(A wave of anguish washes over* **TOM JR**. *He bites it back.)*

Just tryin'...do my best but...thangs get real outta hand real fast, you know?

OSSIE. Yessir. I do.

TOM JR. Listen, friend. I'm gon' tell you somethin' for yo' own good. Those northern fellas...they be in real trouble. One what's in jail...he may not be there too much longer. And there just ain't...gonna be nothin' none of us can do...

OSSIE. What do you mean, sir?

TOM JR. I... *(Beat.)* No...no, you nevermind. You just get home fast and in a hurry. You understands?

> *(***OSSIE*** *studies* **TOM JR**. *cautiously. Then continues his illusion of cutting through the yard.)*

OSSIE. Sho' nuff, sir.

> *(***TOM JR**. *curiously watches him for a moment.)*

TOM JR. And fella... If'n you see that runaway, you let 'im know to get on outta town quick...'fore he catches a fate like his friend. Law is on his tail...and if'n he stick around, he ain't makin' it outta Natchez alive. You make sho' to tell him that...if'n you happen to see him up the road.

> *(***OSSIE*** *stops and looks at* **TOM JR**. *peculiarly.* **TOM JR**. *stares at* **OSSIE** *knowingly.)*

OSSIE. Hear tell that fella got steel nerves. Don't scare too easy. Now if I see him up the road, I'll be sure to pass on your message. But don't know if it'll turn him around. Might be...whatdya say? One of them...ornery ones... *(Beat.)* 'Nite sir.

> *(***OSSIE*** *tips his hat and walks out of the yard.* **TOM JR**. *watches after him...)*
>
> *(Blackout.)*

End of Act I

ACT II

Scene One

(Midnight falls on the yard. **OSSIE** *re-enters, looking around carefully. When he's sure he's clear, he pulls out a cigarette, lights it, and sits on the steps for a puff. Long drag.)*

(He pulls out a small switchblade and flips it. In the dirt, he carves his initials aimlessly.)

*(***NA ROSE** *enters in the darkness, bustling with her keys, unaware of* **OSSIE.** *He hears the jangling and raises his blade toward her quickly.)*

(They both see each other and **NA ROSE** *gasps.)*

NA ROSE. Oh!

OSSIE. Oh! Sorry miss! Couldn't tell it was you!

*(***OSSIE** *quickly closes the blade and pockets it.)*

You alright?

NA ROSE. Scared me half to death!

OSSIE. I apologize. Just havin' a midnight smoke.

NA ROSE. Watcha doin' with that thang anyway?

OSSIE. Protection.

NA ROSE. Shouldn't be out here like this. 'Spose to be in the backhouse.

OSSIE. Just havin' a quick smoke before I head inside. Man needs his vice. *(Beat.)* I'm keepin' watch. Don't you fret.

> (**OSSIE** *sits back on the stair and lights another smoke.*)

> (**NA ROSE** *watches him quietly. He returns her stare.*)

Comin' in late yourself tonight, aren't ya?

NA ROSE. Had some thangs to tend to...

OSSIE. I see...late night things...

NA ROSE. Not them kinda thangs.

OSSIE. You mean things like juke joints. Blues. Whiskey. Those kinda things?

NA ROSE. Perhaps.

OSSIE. Well you shoulda told me. I'd hate to miss a chance to see Ravishing Rose in action.

NA ROSE. You're makin' fun!

OSSIE. Maybe a lil'...

> (**OSSIE** *smiles.* **NA ROSE** *takes a moment.*)

NA ROSE. Wasn't much action from me no how. Just like to sneak out after Ainee sleep sometimes and watch them blues bands. Sang along. Mostly pretendin' is all I do. All I'm ever gon' do really. Fool dreamin'...

OSSIE. Only way a dream is a fool dream is if you leave it be and never follow it. That's the only way.

> (**OSSIE** *holds out his cig.*)

You wanna sit? Share one?

NA ROSE. Oh naw. Naw. That ain't my vice.

OSSIE. What is your vice?

NA ROSE. Wouldn't you like to know...

(She smiles slyly. **OSSIE** *is intrigued.)*

Moon is full tonight. Stars blanketing the sky.

OSSIE. Yeah, it is. *(Beat.)* I like how you put things. Real gentle and soft.

(A moment.)

It's a real thing of beauty tonight.

NA ROSE. You still talkin' 'bout the stars?

OSSIE. Nope.

(OSSIE *smiles flirtatiously.)*

(Beat.)

NA ROSE. You just gonna stay there smokin' and blockin' the door all night?

OSSIE. Oh, my mistake.

(OSSIE *slides over on the step and puts out his cig.)*

I'll move outta your way so you can get on inside.

NA ROSE. Who says I was goin' inside just now?

OSSIE. Well where else are you goin'?

(NA ROSE *walks over and sits on the steps.)*

NA ROSE. Hmph.

(OSSIE *laughs.)*

OSSIE. That your favorite word?

NA ROSE. What's that?

OSSIE. *(Mocking her.)* Hmph!

NA ROSE. Tell me true... You really gonna get us votin'?

OSSIE. I'm gonna damn try.

NA ROSE. Ain't you scared to the dickens 'bout what could happen to you?

OSSIE. Got no time to be scared.

NA ROSE. Tha's all you got to say?

OSSIE. What else to say? I can't be thinking too much about fear. It's nothing but an illusion. Stand in front of you and try to stop you from doing what you know inside is right. I rather try to do something than sit back and let this Jim Crow keep telling me I'm not fit to be nothing more than a boot-licker. I have me a college degree. And when I come down here, White man who's got no education still thinking himself better than me. I wait 'til fear disappears before I take my shot at equality, I'll be waiting 'til I die.

NA ROSE. Where your folks? What they think 'bout all this?

OSSIE. Where yours?

NA ROSE. Gone. Dead I 'spose.

OSSIE. Mine too. *(Beat.)* My paw got killed when I was a young'un. Got himself upset with some White men he sold property to. Cheated him out of his full penance. Went down to where those men were and demanded his pay. Never saw him alive after that. Found his body in the river behind an empty barge. *(Beat.)* Where yours?

NA ROSE. Just dead. *(Beat.)* You gots you some kinda ambition. Real prideful, you are.

OSSIE. Say I'm just like my paw. Folks say his pride got him killed. Don't know what my fate's gonna be yet. *(Shift.)* You have some kinda ambition yourself, don't you? Writing your own songs and all. Gonna make you a fine blues woman.

NA ROSE. Maybe not. Ainee say blues ain't nothin' but despair. Whatever it supposed to be, way down deep in the soul that get you singin' it right...guessin' I ain't got it yet.

OSSIE. Oh I think you got it. *(Beat.)* Say, if you don't mind me asking...what're you doing in a place like this? I can tell you're not like those other women.

NA ROSE. How can you tell?

OSSIE. Just can. I've been scratchin' my head around this whole place. Grateful for the stay, mind you. But still can't figure out for my life why a Negro woman would run a business like this...segregated and all...just isn't right.

NA ROSE. *(Offended.)* Well let me tell you, you don't know everythang, you ornery northern boy. Come down judgin' us that way ain't right. Ainee a good woman with a troubled past. And I ain't too interested in listenin' to you bad mouth her. Good night.

OSSIE. I'm sorry...didn't mean to offend –

NA ROSE. I say you rude. Said it first day I met you and still sayin' it.

> (**NA ROSE** *gets up in a huff and starts to go inside.* **OSSIE** *stands and catches her hand, gently. She is stopped by the touch. Startled but electrified.)*

OSSIE. I'm sorry...don't leave. I didn't mean to upset you. I...

> *(Beat.* **NA ROSE** *stay frozen...hesitant to leave.* **OSSIE** *looks at her.)*

You've been good company to me. Please?

> (**NA ROSE** *considers. Then finally, she returns.)*

NA ROSE. Thangs 'bout a woman be complicated and messy most times, Mr. Brown.

OSSIE. So I see. My apologies.

> *(A moment of quiet. They search for the next words. Beat.)*

You know where you oughta be with a voice like yours? New York City. Chicago. Detroit. You ever been up north?

NA ROSE. Never.

OSSIE. That's where I'm heading next. Gonna go maybe work for the N-A-A-C-P. Start my own office, even. Blackbottom Detroit – Paradise Valley...a place where the blues is played. Where Negroes have their own business and land. You ever heard of it?

NA ROSE. *(Laughing.)* Up north? The blues? You sound as green as that grass in the mornin'! This here's Mississippi. The Delta got the onliest blues there is.

OSSIE. Says who?

NA ROSE. Blues say so itself.

OSSIE. Anywhere Negro folks go, the blues follow.

NA ROSE. Says who?

OSSIE. Says...the Negro.

> *(**NA ROSE** and **OSSIE** laugh. Chuckle. Smile. Stare into each other's faces. **OSSIE** is close enough to smell her skin. He subtly inhales.)*

You smell like...jasmine...

NA ROSE. You smell like...cigarettes...

OSSIE. You ever been kissed?

NA ROSE. *(Embarrassed.)* 'Course.

> *(**OSSIE** studies her simplicity. Her doubt.)*

OSSIE. May I?

> (**NA ROSE** *shrugs shyly. He takes her head in his hands and kisses her softly.*)

> (*He pulls away slowly and studies her.*)

You alright?

NA ROSE. You?

OSSIE. I'd be better if I heard that sweet voice of yours again. Will you sing me a song?

NA ROSE. You ain't hear it?

OSSIE. Hear what?

NA ROSE. That blues.

OSSIE. (*Smiling.*) Maybe I should give another listen.

> (**OSSIE** *leans in to kiss her again. She kisses back passionately.*)

Sweet blues. I heard it real nice. Ravishing Rose indeed.

NA ROSE. I best be gettin' inside now 'fore somebody wake up.

OSSIE. Surely. I best too...

> (**OSSIE** *stands and moves away from the door.*)

Maybe I see you tomorrow...same time? Be nice to have your company.

NA ROSE. Maybe. (*She winks.*) Be careful out there, Mr. Brown.

OSSIE. I think you can call me Ossie now.

NA ROSE. I think I can too... (*Smiles.*) 'Nite.

> (**OSSIE** *stares after* **NA ROSE** *for a lingering moment. She disappears into the house.*)

(Lights crossfade to the common room.)

(**NELLIE** *sits at the jukebox, thumbing through the tunes.*)

(**NA ROSE** *stops – startled at the sight of* **NELLIE**. **NELLIE** *doesn't look at her.*)

Ainee? What you doin' up?

NELLIE. Couldn't sleep. *(Beat.)* Where you been?

NA ROSE. I...was just...out gettin' a late bite. Just gettin' back with Rollo not too long ago. Had lotta traffic on the road back from Louisiana.

(**NELLIE** *looks at her. Skeptical.*)

NELLIE. That so?

NA ROSE. Yes, that's so. *(Beat.)* I better get on to bed now. Got breakfast to make early...

NELLIE. You know the thang 'bout this jukebox, Rose?

NA ROSE. What's that Ainee?

NELLIE. I think what that man tellin' Rollo was right. It must got the haunts.

NA ROSE. Why you say that?

NELLIE. Just get a funny feelin' when I listen to it. Say the man what sold it to Rollo lost his wife some months prior, and just filled the catalogue with blues. And sometimes when it be late at night, say the man could hear the box playin' by itself. He go to check the chord and it be unplugged. Man had himself a nervous breakdown not long after that. I thinkin' a piece of his wife must be in this box. Got her haunts. Maybe other haunts too. *(Beat.)* I worry 'bout you Rose.

NA ROSE. I'm fine Ainee. Ain't nothin' to worry 'bout me for.

NELLIE. I worry 'bout you cuz you young and pretty and full of influence. You ain't had to pay no costs. And I hopin' you don't have to. *(Beat.)* I don't wants you out no mo'. Late at night. You hearin' me?

    (Beat.)

NA ROSE. But Ainee...

NELLIE. Don't get swooped up in the wrong winds, Rose... some ain't headin' for nothin' but a hurricane.

    *(**NA ROSE** is silent. Looks at **NELLIE** defiantly.)*

NA ROSE. I... *(Pause / shift.)* See you in mornin' Ainee.

    (She turns and disappears into the rooms.)

    *(**NELLIE** remains behind. Plays a tune on the jukebox*. Lights shift.)*

Scene Two

(The tune of Albina Jones' "Evil Gal Blues"*
plays from the jukebox.)

*(**MARLA** at the bar, pours herself some brandy*
and sings along off-key but unashamed in
her drunkeness.)

(The back door to the house closes.)

*(**REE ANN** enters the common room. Sees*
***MARLA** in action. Instantly agitated.)*

*(**NA ROSE** and **SANDY** enter shortly after.)*

SANDY. Marl, we picked of them good strawberries you
like at the –

> *(**SANDY** stops and gasps at **MARLA** who*
> *continues singing.)*

MARLA. Welcome home gals. Have some brandy with me,
won'tcha?

SANDY. Marl, that Nellie's good brandy?! Has you gone
mad?!

> *(**REE ANN** goes over to the jukebox and pulls*
> *the plug.)*

---

* A license to produce *Follow Me to Nellie's* does not include a
performance license for "Evil Gal Blues." The publisher and author
suggest that the licensee contact ASCAP or BMI to ascertain the
music publisher and contact such music publisher to license or acquire
permission for performance of the song. If a license or permission
is unattainable for "Evil Gal Blues," the licensee may not use the song
in *Follow Me to Nellie's* but should create an original composition in
a similar style or use a similar song in the public domain. For further
information, please see the Music and Third Party Materials Use Note
on page iii.

MARLA. Ree Ann I was listenin' to that!

REE ANN. Stop it Marl. You drunk.

SANDY. Nellie be back from town soon. Best she not see you this way.

MARLA. I don't give a rat's ass 'bout no Nellie seein' me no kinda way. Even Nellie Jackson can't get my spirits down today. She can go to shit for all I care.

REE ANN. Leave it 'lone, Marl.

MARLA. Have one lil' drink with me, won'tcha Sandy? To celebrate.

SANDY. Celebrate what, Marl?

MARLA. Ree Ann, ain't you told her?! Jim done got discharged. He comin' for me. Sent me telegram sayin' so. Ree Ann done read the whole thang for me.

REE ANN. I say leave it 'lone!

> (**REE ANN** *snatches the glass from* **MARLA**'s *hand.*)

SANDY. Where that ballplayer Marl? You 'spose to be here layin' wit' 'im. Ain't that why you ain't come to the market?

MARLA. Told him to get the hell on.

> (**REE ANN** *looks at* **MARLA**'s *face. Bruised.*)

REE ANN. What done happened to yo' face?

MARLA. Callin' me outta my name. I tole' him he bet not and he did it anyway.

SANDY. Callin' you how?

MARLA. Ain't civilized. I tole' him to cut it and he wouldn't. So's I spit in his face and told him to run on!

REE ANN. Marla, gotdamn! Say you ain't!

SANDY. He hurt you?

MARLA. Nobody callin' me outta my name. No mo'. It's a new day for Marl. Ain't gonna be here another night. Goin' to meet my Jim at the train station this evenin'. Gonna surprise him – lookin' my best.

SANDY. That for true?

MARLA. Tolja I ain't got to lie 'bout nothin'. Been two years already since we said our so-longs, but I knew the day would come where we gets a chance to start over. And it here, right now.

> (**MARLA** *moves sloppily over to* **NA ROSE** *and leans against her.*)

Where my shawl, Lil' Bit? I needs it now. I done paid you full.

NA ROSE. It's...finished... I...just lemme go grab it for you...

MARLA. Gonna wear it nice and pretty for Jim. Look like the lady he rememberin' me to be.

> (**REE ANN** *pulls* **MARLA** *away from* **NA ROSE.** **NA ROSE** *runs off to the rooms.*)

REE ANN. Go get yaself cleaned up. Nellie ain't gonna believe your tale over that ballplayer's with that liquor on your breath. It's 'gainst the rules – that liquor. You know that much.

MARLA. I look like I'm thankin' 'bout some gotdamn rules?

REE ANN. Marla, Nellie done give you a warnin'. You mess up one mo' time and you out by the riverboat. You listenin' good? Down by that riverboat where them hoes get all kinds of johns hittin' 'em and smakin' 'em 'round. Even killin' 'em. Like that one – whasshername?

SANDY. (*Shivering.*) That Tessa.

REE ANN. Found her body in the river, Marl. Say them

White boys did a good number on her 'fore they stabbed her up good. That ain't no life for no kinda Colored woman. Not even one livin' as a whore. Nellie give us a better chance at livin' than that. You keep steppin' foolish you gone mess up all you got!

MARLA. This ain't all I got! You speaks fo' yaself! I knows you don't believe me none, Ree Ann, but I'm gone. Tonight. You likes it or not.

> (MARLA *goes back over to the jukebox and looks for songs.* NA ROSE *enters with a gorgeous knitted shawl. It is long and flowing. The colors are woven together in golds and silvers. It is regal.*)

SANDY. Wowee! Thas for Marla?

NA ROSE. Sho' nuff. Took me a while, I know. But this here pattern was somethin' kinda tricky. Had to re-do it 'bout ten times 'fore I got it all right.

> (NA ROSE *walks over to* MARLA *to present the shawl.* MARLA *picks up the shawl, touches it against her cheek. Enjoys it for a moment.*)
>
> (*Then, abruptly, as if she remembered her hatred, she throws the shawl on the floor.*)

REE ANN. Marla!

MARLA. I hate it.

> (NA ROSE – *shattered, stares at* MARLA *in disgust.*)

SANDY. Marla!

MARLA. I say I hate it. It's ugly. I wants my money back.

NA ROSE. (*Broken.*) Fine by me.

> (NA ROSE *digs into her pockets and pulls out*

> *one dollar in coins. She throws the money at*
> **MARLA**.)

One dollar. Take it!

> (**MARLA** *squares off to* **NA ROSE**
> *threateningly.*)

MARLA. You throw somethin' at Marla you best be ready to
get laid out on this ground! You hear me!

> (**MARLA** *lunges for* **NA ROSE**. **REE ANN**
> *between them and holds* **MARLA** *off.*)

REE ANN. No Marl. No!

> (*The back door to the house slams.*)

> (**REE ANN** *pulls* **MARLA** *back as the women*
> *compose themselves – frantic and breathless.*)

> (**NELLIE** *enters the common room. Stillness.*)

> (*She looks around the room. Walks over to*
> **MARLA** *slowly. Stands before her. Silence.*)

> (*In an instant, she slaps* **MARLA** *harshly*
> *across the face.*)

NELLIE. Spittin' in a White man's face. Done lost your God-
fearin' mind. You tryin' to make me lose my business?
My customers? You best get on your knees and beg that
man don't call the law on this house. You hears me?!
Go'on down to him this evenin'. And if'n you decide
not to, you pack yo' bags and get outta this house befo'
daybreak. That's all to it.

> (**NELLIE** *turns to walk away.*)

> (**MARLA** *touches her stinging cheek.*)

MARLA. (*Low and deliberate.*) What kinda Colored woman
is you?

REE ANN. Marl...

> (**NELLIE** *stops. Turns back to* **MARLA.**)

MARLA. Treatin' us like yo' dog food. These White mens? Least that's how they come from the start. Ain't had nothin' to know different. But you??? Come from the same root. And still ain't treatin' us no better. Jim Crow out there. Jim Crow in here.

NELLIE. Get outta my house Marl.

MARLA. This whole south got newness comin', and way you carry on, Negroes stay scrapin' the bottom of it all.

> (**NELLIE** *walks over to* **MARLA** *calmly.*)

NELLIE. You don't like the ways of thangs, leave 'em.

MARLA. I'm is.

NELLIE. This here ain't no paradise. Ain't no equal rights. Ain't no holy land. You wants to be baptized and cleanse yo' soul, you in the wrong damn place. You want justice? You in the wrong damn place. This work ain't for promise of tomorrows. It for gettin' through the day. It ain't for the ones still lookin' for where they is. It for the ones who know they already gone and ain't comin' back. You still tryin' to get your piece at life? Leave, I say! Leave and go straight to Heaven or Hell – whichever you can find. But don't come lookin' at me to be somethin' better than the rest of the whole goddamned south. Cuz that ain't what this is. That just ain't what this is.

MARLA. *(With gravity.)* I'm leavin'. For good. And I ain't comin' back.

NELLIE. Well good for ya –

> (*A cough overtakes* **NELLIE.** *It is harsh and violent.*)

NA ROSE. Ainee! You alright?

REE ANN. Get her some tea!

SANDY. I'll do it. Go put a pot on right now.

> (**SANDY** *heads into the kitchen.*)

NELLIE. *(To* **MARLA,** *sincerely.)* Good for ya...

> (**NA ROSE** *helps* **NELLIE** *off right behind her.*)

> (**REE ANN** *looks at* **MARLA,** *who hangs on by a thread.*)

> (*She walks up to her, and touches her face tenderly.*)

REE ANN. Gon' get you cleaned up Marl. Take down that swellin'. Don't you worry. 'Kay?

MARLA. Thank he'll still want me, Ree Ann? If I covers up good? Still look like somethin'?

> (*Beat.* **REE ANN** *looks at* **MARLA** *for a second.*)

REE ANN. Marl... *(Hesitates / beat.)* I thank you gonna be a real sight.

> (**MARLA**'s *face in* **REE ANN**'s *hands. She registers the feeling for a moment.*)

> (*Then* **MARLA** *pulls away and heads to the rooms.*)

> (*Long silence.* **REE ANN** *watches after for a thoughtful moment. The finally exits behind her.*)

> (*Beat.*)

> (**ROLLO** *enters the yard hastily. Opens the door and peers in.*)

ROLLO. Nellie! Nellie you here?!

(**NELLIE** *enters from the kitchen.*)

NELLIE. Rollo – what's all that fussin'?

ROLLO. They took him, Nellie.

NELLIE. Took who?

ROLLO. Eli. They stole him from the jailhouse.

NELLIE. Lord, no. You sho'?

ROLLO. They come to us while we down at the school, waitin' for Ossie to show. He 'sposin to meet us there and then we go over to the courthouse. But he never show. Vernon Boys come instead. Come askin' us Ossie's whereabouts and we ain't say. So they try to rough us up a bit. Twisted my arm behind my back real good.

> (**NELLIE** *goes to* **ROLLO** *and tries to help him settle.*)

NELLIE. Got to sit you down and get you tended to.

ROLLO. Ain't no time for that. Got to find Ossie. Just checked for him at the backhouse and he ain't there. Them Vernon Boys gonna make a mess of things Nellie. That's what they promisin'.

> (**SANDY** *and* **NA ROSE** *enter. They stop at the urgency in the room.*)

NA ROSE. *(Softly.)* What done happened?

ROLLO. Nellie, if'n Ossie ain't here and he ain't there –

SANDY. That Mr. Brown be missin'?

> (**NELLIE** *looks at* **NA ROSE**.)

NELLIE. You ain't seen him...has you Rose?

> (**NA ROSE** *is jarred for a moment.*)

NA ROSE. Me? *(Breathless.)* No...

ROLLO. I got to go find him.

NELLIE. I go on down to Sheriff Toms. See if he can't do
nothin' 'bout Eli.

SANDY. I go tell the gals!

> (**SANDY** *runs off to the rooms.* **NELLIE** *grabs
> a shawl and heads to the door.* **ROLLO** *right
> behind her.* **NELLIE** *stops suddenly.*)

NELLIE. Eli's family... I... *(Beat.)* Rollo, we got to find 'em.
And Rose...if'n that Mr. Brown comes back here, you
keep him. You keep him however you gots to. *(Pause.)*
Good God...

> (**NELLIE** *leaves...* **ROLLO** *two steps behind.*)

> (**NA ROSE** *stays put, alone... Breathless...*)

Scene Three

(The sound of crickets hum in the yard. The common room is barely lit, save for a small lamp at the end table. **NA ROSE** *sits on the couch waiting for* **OSSIE**. *She checks the door periodically. Restless.)*

(A small noise in the yard. The sound of a sodapop can being kicked. **NA ROSE** *rushes over to the side door and sees* **OSSIE** *crouching in the darkness.)*

NA ROSE. In here! Quick-like!

*(***OSSIE*** scurries inside the common room, dirty and disheveled. He walks over to the couch and plops down with exhaustion. Wipes blood from his temple.)*

Keep quiet. The gals' asleep. *(Looks at his face.)* Lawd. You been hurt.

(She touches his wound gently.)

OSSIE. *(Wincing.)* Ssssssstttttttttttt...

NA ROSE. Sorry! Let me just get somethin'...

(She walks over to the kitchen and grabs a wet towel. Comes back over to **OSSIE**, *and tends to his wounds.)*

Who put a hurtin' on you?

OSSIE. Couple of fellas, came up on me when I was on my way down to the school. Wanted to know where I was headed. I wouldn't tell 'em. So we got into a tussle. They doubled up on me. One of 'em must've had knuckles made of brass. Hurt like hell.

NA ROSE. Lawd, they coulda killed ya.

OSSIE. A Negro man looking on – he come out. Shot a rifle
in the air, and the fellas run off. He told me to get outta
there. Wouldn't let me inside. Too dangerous, he say.
Told me to take the backwoods. Been hidin' and makin'
my way back here as best I could.

> (**NA ROSE** *touches him softly. Holds his face*
> *in her hands and studies him lovingly.*)

NA ROSE. You been through hell...

OSSIE. I got off easy. Everybody else going through hell.
Because of me. *(Pause.)* It's my fault.

NA ROSE. Shhh now... Don't you fuss...

OSSIE. It's my fault, I tell you. I pushed for this Rose.
Pushed for us to come here to do this drive. Said to
Eli, look what this Reverend Lee did. Getting Negroes
to vote in these southern counties. If we can get
equal rights going in the south, we can do anything.
Work for any Negro organization we want. And now
he's missing from that jail, and folks are in trouble...
because of me.

NA ROSE. What happened to him wun'nt yo' doin'.

OSSIE. And it wasn't my un-doing either. They told me.
The older ones in the Council. They told me to be
prepared for Mississippi. The blood here spills fast
and long. They told me, don't dive in the waters. Dip
in slowly. But I just... I got down here and I didn't feel
like moving backwards. I've been educated around my
own people. Seen Negro professors – distinguished and
proud. Well read and forward thinkers. I've seen what
the other side of the line is, and when I look down here
at these Negroes, bowing their heads and saying "yes
suh" and "no suh" to these Whites who don't have a lick
of education, it makes my skin itch. Makes me feel –

NA ROSE. Feel what?

OSSIE. I don't want to say.

NA ROSE. 'Shamed of us?

> *(Silence.)*

OSSIE. I know I shouldn't think so, Rose. I know it's wrong of me. But sometimes...maybe.

> *(**NA ROSE** pulls away.)*

I've offended you again. I'm –

NA ROSE. Rollo and Mr. Pete was nothin' but proud to be in that river with you. And maybe they ain't been able to get all what you done got, but don't make 'em any less of somethin'. Makes 'em courageous, I thank. It take a real kinda strength to live this way and still got the will to work for somethin' better.

OSSIE. You're right, Rose. I know it. *(Pause.)* This pride in me...it's nothing but foolish.

NA ROSE. You don't believe that.

OSSIE. I do. I used to think it was worth something. Willing to fight for it, even. But now I see...pride will only get you killed. Just like my paw.

NA ROSE. Not yo' kinda pride. Yo' kinda pride what get people believin' in theyselves. Get people thankin' they got some kinda dreams worth fightin' for. Only way a dream is a fool dream is if you leave it be and never follow it. Ain't that what you sayin' to me? Was that nothin' but talk? Cuz it shoul' felt like somethin' real to me. Held onto it.

> *(**OSSIE** looks at **NA ROSE** with complete surrender.)*

OSSIE. Rose, you remember that night you asked me if I was afraid. You remember that?

NA ROSE. Yeah.

OSSIE. I wasn't all the way truthful with you.

NA ROSE. You wun'nt?

OSSIE. Today, taking those backwoods...this terrible feeling came over me. Looking at that red dirt...the rocks on the roads...it felt like I could disappear at any minute and it wouldn't matter to anybody at all. Wouldn't matter how much education I had. Wouldn't matter where I come from. I could just disappear somewhere with those rocks and that dirt and just be a Negro man that got buried in Mississippi. Another Negro man. No name. No history. Nobody to love and be survived by. And that Rose...that thought...that scared me to the bone.

NA ROSE. Nothin' wrong wit' a lil' fear, I thank. But you some kinda courage, too. Cuz you coulda run. Could leave all this behind. And you ain't. You here, pushin' us to that river 'til we all swimmin' in our rights. That's a good kinda pride, I thank.

OSSIE. I say... I like how you put things. Soft. *(Pause. He touches her face.)* Like your skin...

> (**NA ROSE** *leans into* **OSSIE**. *They kiss. Beat. He pulls away.*)

Will you sing me a song?

NA ROSE. It's late!

OSSIE. Just a little hum.

NA ROSE. The gals...they's sleepin'...

OSSIE. Just somethin' soft. To soothe me? Say you will.

> *(Beat.* **NA ROSE** *sighs. She thinks for a moment, stroking his head. Softly, she begins a tune.)*

NA ROSE.
ROLL LIKE A STONE
YOUR HEART IN MY HANDS

ROLL IN WITH THE TIDE
MY BLUES MAN
TAKE ME TO THE RIVER
TAKE ME TO THE SANDS
TAKE ME ANYWHERE
MY BLUES MAN*

(Beat.)

That's all I 'member…

OSSIE. Pretty… *(Beat.)* You made that up yourself?

NA ROSE. Was hopin' to maybe…take it on the road. But… my dreams ain't really possible.

OSSIE. Oh they possible. You made for singin' us to healing… Ain't not a soul could do it better than Ravishing Rose…

NA ROSE. I like how you put thangs.

(He smiles. She kisses him.)

*(***TOM JR.*** enters into the yard and approaches the door. He knocks.)*

*(***OSSIE*** and **NA ROSE** look up, startled.)*

Who come knockin' here so late?

OSSIE. Could be Rollo looking for me.

NA ROSE. You best git off in that kitchen and stay quiet. I'll check.

*(***OSSIE*** nods and disappears into the kitchen. **NA ROSE** creeps over to the side door and halts when she sees **TOM JR**. She doesn't open.)*

---

* A license to produce *Follow Me to Nellie's* does not include a performance license for any third-party or copyrighted music. Licensees should create an original melody. For further information, please see the Music and Third Party Materials Use Note on page iii.

TOM JR. Evenin', Miss. Sorry to bother ya so late an' all.

NA ROSE. Nellie out right now, sir. Tell her you been by and have her call ya first thang in the mornin'.

TOM JR. Yes, I knows. She's down talkin' to Pop. But well… *(He hesitates.)* May I come in for a quick sec?

> (**NA ROSE** *pauses in a moment of judgment. She looks uneasy.*)

Don't mean to put ya out, miss. It's just…a bit windy out here tonight. Think a storm's approachin'…

> (**NA ROSE** *hesitantly opens the side door and lets* **TOM JR.** *in.*)

Just doin' my rounds here on Rankin Street. Nobody's been by here botherin' ya or causin' trouble, has they?

NA ROSE. No sir. Everythang's been alright here.

TOM JR. Checkin' on folks since that Eli's gone missing.

NA ROSE. Yessir. Thank you.

TOM JR. But don't you folks worry. My pop is on top of those Vernon Boys. They've been causing trouble for lotsa folk…not just Coloreds. Miss Tompkins accused 'em of stealin' her pocketbook right outta her pouch last week. Some Whites just give the rest of us a bad look to people. But we ain't all that unreasonable.

> (**NA ROSE** *is quiet.* **TOM JR.** *moves closer to her. Carefully.*)

I wun'nt raised in no kinda dislike for Coloreds. Hear tell them folks up north sayin' all kinds of thangs 'gainst us southern Whites, but we ain't all born with that hate in us. Thas why I been keepin' that votin' fella safe. Been keepin' the mobs clear of him. I know it… Know he stayin' 'round here. Seen him once, I did. But I ain't sayin' nothin'. Just wants to give 'im a chance to leave quiet-like. Believes me you. It hurts me to see thangs like what happened that Till fella much as it hurts ya'll. Don't wanna see nothin' like that happen here. I had all kinds a nightmares after picturin' him in that casket. Terrible what some folks'll do to others. Terrible.

> *(Pause.* **NA ROSE** *remains quiet, watching* **TOM JR**. *with intense caution. He inhales her beauty.)*

I remembers where I've seen ya before.

> *(***NA ROSE*** *looks at him nervously.)*

NA ROSE. I think you have me mistaken, sir.

TOM JR. I remembers. I 'membered first night I saw ya here. Saw ya in Nawlins one night. You was leavin' that Co Co Club on Bourbon Street what play the blues. Seen Albinia Jones there that night. Sangin' like her soul was movin' through the crowd. And I seen you.

NA ROSE. I tell ya, it wasn't me, sir.

TOM JR. 'Course it was. It was you. Tellin' ya, you was sangin' to yaself out there under that street lamp. I remembers, cuz I thought you was real purrty. Look like a gal I used to have somethin' with couple years back. Negro gal. Mayleen. Her skin was smooth as oil, it was. And her lips was fuller than I ever had known before. She was somethin' of a gal. Even loved her, I did. Never tole' her, but I did. *(Beat.)* When her paw found out what we had, he beat her, he did. Beat her 'til her brain swole. Beat her 'til she was gone. I lost her, I did. *(Beat.)* When I saw you down there on Bourbon Street, lookin' like the spittin' image of my gal... I just... ain't knowed what to say to you. Like seein' a ghost. I knowed then you must be...somethin' awfully special too...

> *(Beat.)*

NA ROSE. Well sir –

TOM JR. You can call me Tom.

NA ROSE. Mr. Tom, sir, it's mighty late.

TOM JR. Yes, miss...you don't mind me askin' – what is your name?

NA ROSE. Name's... Na Rose, sir...

>   (**TOM JR.** *moves closer to* **NA ROSE**...
>   *cautiously...but needfully...*)

TOM JR. I like that name... Na Rose...like the flower...

NA ROSE. Mr. Tom, I thank I should be goin' off to bed now...

TOM JR. Forgive me askin' but may I...may I just touch your skin –

>   (**TOM JR.** *reaches his arm out to her. She backs*
>   *away sharply.*)

NA ROSE. Mr. Tom –

TOM JR. I don't wanna hurt ya or nothin'...promise...

>   (**NA ROSE** *backs away more definitely...looks*
>   *at the gun on his hip. He follows her eyes.*)

Oh don't be 'fraid of that. I won't use it on ya. I promise. Don't like to use it no way.

>   (*He pulls off the gun slowly and places it on*
>   *the table. He advances to* **NA ROSE**.)

See? Just...wanna touch you gentle-like...

NA ROSE. Mr. Tom, please –

TOM JR. You just...so much like her...

>   (**TOM JR.** *advances to* **NA ROSE** *needfully.*
>   *Mechanically. Almost outside of himself.*)

(**NA ROSE** *lay stuck between him and the cabinets, unable to back any further.*)

NA ROSE. Mr. Tom, no!

TOM JR. Just want to feel her again –

NA ROSE. No!

TOM JR. Promise I won't hurt ya none. I promise –

(**TOM JR**. *leans in to touch* **NA ROSE**'s *face. Startled, she screams and tries to push him.*)

NA ROSE. I say NO!

TOM JR. Okay I'm sorry. You don't have to be 'fraid –

(**NA ROSE** *screams.*)

(**OSSIE** *rushes out of the kitchen.*)

(*With one sweep, he pulls* **TOM JR**. *away from* **NA ROSE** *and knocks him sharply to the floor.*)

(**NA ROSE** *shakes with anger and tears.*)

(**TOM JR**. *is stunned. He looks at* **OSSIE** *and tries to make sense of everything.*)

(*Recognizing.*) You...

OSSIE. Time for you to leave, sir.

TOM JR. Crazy...

(**OSSIE** *notices* **TOM JR**.'s *gun.* **TOM JR**. *raises to his feet to grab his gun.* **OSSIE** *beats him to it and holds the gun out to* **TOM JR**.)

OSSIE. I say, time for you to leave, sir.

(**TOM JR**. *stay stunned. He backs away slowly to the door and looks once more at the sight* *that is* **NA ROSE** *and* **OSSIE**.*)*

(In a painful attempt to regroup himself...)

TOM JR. Thas gonna cost you...nigger.

*(***TOM JR.*** storms out into the night.)*

*(***OSSIE*** and* **NA ROSE** *look after* **TOM JR.** *wordlessly.)*

(They look at each other. Speechless.)

(Blackout.)

Scene Four

*(**NA ROSE** sits on the couch as **SANDY** pats her hands.)*

*(**OSSIE** stands by the door and keeps watch. Tom Jr.'s gun in his hand.)*

SANDY. That tea be my best mix, I thank. Put a lil' pinch of brown sugar in with the honey and the lemon. Make it extra sweet tastin' so it go down with a touch of joy.

*(**NA ROSE** doesn't sip. Her gaze stay on **OSSIE**, who gazes out of the window with concern.)*

Ain't you likin' it?

NA ROSE. Not thirsty much.

*(**REE ANN** enters from the kitchen.)*

REE ANN. Rung Nellie down at the jailhouse. She and Rollo on they way back with the truck soon. Say everybody stay put 'til then.

(Momentary silence.)

SANDY. That Mr. Tom wanted to touch some skin, he had plenty here to choose from. Ain't he?

REE ANN. That ain't the kinda skin he wanted. That fella got haunts in 'im. That gal he say he missin'...she must got some kinda hold on him. Ain't no tellin' what un-godliness he done seen firsthand, but he must got haunts on 'im fa sho'.

(Another pause.)

Mr. Brown, Nellie want you all packed when they get here. Hit the roads faster.

OSSIE. They find Eli?

REE ANN. Ain't say. But she meanin' it Mr. Brown. Say it time for you to go. Her voice sounded final with the truth.

OSSIE. I'll talk to her, just the same.

(*Pause.*)

SANDY. Marla ain't come back. Wun'nt in her bed. Guessin' she tellin' the truth this time 'bout Jim. Done run off with him for good.

REE ANN. That kinda truth ain't never final.

SANDY. She ain't even say goodbye. Guessin' part of me hopin' she come back just so's I can hug her one mo'gin. But then other part of me hopin' she don't never come back. For the sake of her heart an' all.

(*Pause. More silence.*)

Na Rose that tea gettin' cold.

(**REE ANN** *watches* **NA ROSE** *watching* **OSSIE**.)

REE ANN. Come on, Sandy. Let's just make another pot. Gonna get the biscuits out too. Somethin' to soak up the nerves swimmin' in all our stomachs.

(**SANDY** *nods – getting the picture. She and* **REE ANN** *head into the kitchen.*)

(**OSSIE** *stay vigilant and alert by the window.* **NA ROSE** *rises from the couch and approaches him. She touches him gently.*)

NA ROSE. What ya gonna do?

OSSIE. Not sure yet.

NA ROSE. You gonna leave?

OSSIE. I...

(*Pause.* **OSSIE** *looks at* **NA ROSE** *softly.*)

...if the Madam wishes.

NA ROSE. Where you gonna go?

OSSIE. Back north. Detroit. Settle with some family there while I look for work.

NA ROSE. Ain't you ever comin' back down?

> *(Pause.)*

OSSIE. Eventually. Got to finish what we started here... eventually.

NA ROSE. Eventually sound like a lifetime away.

OSSIE. I... *(Beat.)* It doesn't have to be.

NA ROSE. I don't wants you to leave.

OSSIE. You can come with me.

NA ROSE. To the north?

OSSIE. Why not? They got blues in Detroit. Paradise Valley got all kinds of places for you to show your pipes. You could really be somethin', Rose – with me.

NA ROSE. What about Ainee? She needin' me here. For the land.

OSSIE. This land? This land is nothing for keeps. Got nothing but Negro blood in its soil. But up north, we got promise. You can be all those things you've been dreaming. Then we come back down when the time is right. Make things better then.

NA ROSE. I... I don't know what to say.

OSSIE. Just say yes.

> **(NA ROSE** *hesitates...confused.)*

> *(Headlights beam into the yard. The sound of an engine roars and stops.)*

This is them.

(**OSSIE** *opens the door and steps into the yard.*
NELLIE *enters, followed by* **ROLLO**. *They are strangely silent.*)

(*A moment.*)

NELLIE. Mr. Brown, you all packed?

OSSIE. If that's your wish, Madam. But I just ask, can it wait until tomorrow. Wanna stick around 'til we go to that courthouse and get everybody registered.

NELLIE. Ain't possible Mr. Brown. I'm sorry but...it just ain't...

(**REE ANN** *and* **SANDY** *enter.*)

SANDY. Nellie, you back. Thank God.

REE ANN. They find Eli?

(*Pause.*)

ROLLO. Tell 'em Nellie.

(**NELLIE** *pauses. Speechless for the first time.*)

(*Sternly.*) You tell 'em.

(*Beat. Weighted and solemn.*)

NELLIE. Eli dead.

| **SANDY**. (*Gasping.*) | **NA ROSE**. |
| Lawd – no. | Oh God. |

NELLIE. They hung him. Front of the courthouse.

NA ROSE. (*Softly.*) No...

REE ANN. (*A whisper.*) God...

NELLIE. We found him. Body – rockin' in the wind. They didn't even have the decency...to cut him down.

(*The room is numb.*)

We didn't make it in time. Went lookin' for the Sheriff and he sayin' he was on the case but...didn't make it in time. Nothin' was in time. He gone. That's what we gon' have to say to his Mama. To his family. We ain't find him. Didn't bail him out. And he gone. *(Beat.)* All that come to me the whole time I'm seein' 'im while the mens cut him down...is wonderin' what kind of casket his mama was gonna choose. Was it gon' be open? Or was she even gon' be able to look at what they done. *(Beat.)* That wun'nt my first time seein' a man that way. But Lawd God, I pray it my last.

> (**ROLLO** *breaks the numbing.*)

ROLLO. We got to get Ossie on the road first thang in the mornin'.

REE ANN. Ain't it better to leave right now?

ROLLO. Roads blocked. Both highways outta Natchez got mens at 'em. Waitin' to catch anyone leavin' the town. They waitin' on us.

NELLIE. Soon as day break, ya'll stand a good chance of gettin' on that highway. For tonight, you stay here. Sleep out in that backhouse with Ossie.

ROLLO. Alright.

NELLIE. You gone need this.

> (**NELLIE** *goes over to the cabinet and pulls out a long rifle. She hands it to* **ROLLO**.)

Just in case.

ROLLO. What about you?

NELLIE. I be fine. Gots me one in my boudoir. I be just fine.

SANDY. What about that Mr. Tom Jr.? He could be makin' his way back here any minute now. What we gon' do?

NELLIE. Ya'll git on to bed. I deal with that Mr. Tom Jr. myself.

ROLLO. Then I stay up witcha.

NELLIE. No Rollo you... *(Pause.)* I gon' handle this by myself.

ROLLO. Nellie.

NELLIE. I got to. I just... I gon' do it myself.

>*(Beat.)*

>*(**NELLIE** coughs vigorously.)*

REE ANN. Nellie you ain't soundin' good. Come let me fix you a cup.

>*(She looks at **NA ROSE**. Looks at **OSSIE**.)*

NELLIE. Alright...

>*(She follows **REE ANN** off. **ROLLO** grabs **OSSIE**'s bag.)*

ROLLO. I load up the truck then. That way we move fast in the morn.

>*(**ROLLO** heads into the yard.)*

SANDY. Come on Na Rose, you can bunk with us tonight. Best not be alone.

NA ROSE. I be up in a bit, Sandy.

>*(**SANDY** exits to the bedrooms as **ROLLO** heads toward the backhouse.)*

>*(**NA ROSE** approaches **OSSIE** slowly.)*

OSSIE. They hung him, Rose.

NA ROSE. I know it.

OSSIE. For me. It was a message to me, Rose. And here I am. Free as a bird.

(**NA ROSE** *touches him again. Softly.*)

NA ROSE. Don't go blamin' yourself again now. For none of it.

OSSIE. You gonna come Rose? Come away with me?

(**NA ROSE** *looks at* **OSSIE**. *Says nothing.*)

Don't answer it. Don't say no. Just sleep on it. Hear me? Sleep on it and I'll hope to see you at the truck in the mornin'.

(**OSSIE** *leans into* **NA ROSE**. *Kisses her like his life depends on it.*)

(*She finally pulls away. A beat.*)

(**OSSIE** *turns to head out.* **NA ROSE** *watches him go with agony...*)

NA ROSE. *(Softly.)* 'Nite...

(*Lights shift.*)

Scene Five

(The gals' room. **REE ANN** *sits up with* **SANDY**.*)*

SANDY. Ree Ann I can't sleep.

REE ANN. Me neither.

SANDY. Can't stop thinkin' of Eli. Don't wanna never see no man hangin'.

REE ANN. Maybe you won't never have to.

SANDY. You seen one befo'?

REE ANN. I has.

SANDY. Who was he? What he done?

REE ANN. Don't know what he done. Didn't matter none. Wouldna made it no better.

(Pause.)

SANDY. You ever think about what it'd be if we was somewhere else? Livin' in another time or county? In the north even? Have a family of some kind. Live without no fear.

REE ANN. Already had a family and they gone now. Don't get to dreamin' 'bout nothin' no mo'. Don't matter where you go, Sandy. You got haunts, they just follow you. Best to give away your dreams and go numb. That way can't nothin' hurt you no mo'. Only way to survive.

(The bedroom door opens. **MARLA** *enters.)*

SANDY. Marl! You home!

*(**MARLA** looks at **REE ANN**, raging.)*

You alright Marl? What happened to ya? Where you been?

REE ANN. *(Knowingly.)* Jim never come Marl. Did he.

MARLA. No Ree Ann. He ain't.

SANDY. Oh Marl…

MARLA. I wait. Wait and wait down at that bus station. Bus with all the vets from Jackson come in and he ain't on it. I gets to wonderin'. So's I take my two nickels – all I gots in my pocket. Give one of 'em to this clerk who was treatin' me pretty nice. Ask her to read my telegram for me again. 'Fraid I musta missed somethin' the first time. So she readin' it to me. But the note ain't quite the same this time. Say he got the metal in his leg – that for true. Say he gettin' discharged – that also for true. Say he comin' back to the states. That for true too. 'Cept it don't say nothin' 'bout comin' back for me. Say he done with Natchez. Ain't nothin' for a Colored here. Done found him a woman live in North Carolina. Gonna be with her and try him a new life up there. But he do say Love. That for true. *(Laughs bitterly.)* Love. Love, Jim. It do say that. Say sorry and good riddens and love. *(Beat.)* That the kinda love I made for, I guess. Goodbye love.

SANDY. Oh Marl… I'm so sorry.

MARLA. You lie Ree Ann. 'Bout what that letter say. Tell me he comin' for me. How come?

*(Pause. **REE ANN** looks at **MARLA** solemnly.)*

REE ANN. You wanted me to, Marl. You wanted to have imaginary. So I give you what you want.

MARLA. That's horse shit Ree Ann, and you know it. Why you lie? Ain't read me that whole letter.

REE ANN. What else you wanted me to do, Marl? You wanted to hear he ain't comin' back from me? You woulda believed me? You woulda done somethin' different? I could tell you Jim wun'nt comin' back. Been tellin' you that all along. I could tell you he just gonna play stickball with yo' feelings but what it matter what I say? Tell me you woulda listened. Tell me you wouldna done everythang the same anyway. Find a way to call me a liar and believe in yo' imaginary. You believed me cuz you wanted to.

MARLA. That a wicked thang you done, Ree Ann. I oughta pound you.

REE ANN. So do it, Marl. Pound me if it make you feel better. I done it so's you see for yourself. Cuz can't nobody tell you nothin' when it come to the heart. Only thang we can do is hand you a mirror. You wanna pound me? Go'on do it. But it ain't gonna take none of that hurtin' away.

> (**MARLA** *stares at* **REE ANN** *fuming. Then suddenly – a break. She weeps.*)

> (**SANDY** *rises up. Touches* **MARLA** *gently. Caresses her.*)

MARLA. Why it can't be for me? The promise of somethin' better? It be for that Na Rose. Why she made for it and I ain't? I'm dyin' here. Can't anybody see?

SANDY. We see, Marl. We see.

> (*She puts her arm around* **MARLA** *warmly.*)

It tryin' to get you Marl. Take ya soul and all ya worthy. (*Beat.*) It don't get me like it get you. Seem like even when I was a gal…bein' touched was just some part of me. Mens always wanted some of it. My smell. My skin. My goodness. Cousins. Boyfriends. Didn't matter. And I learn not to hold it so sacred. Learn that it just the outside…but my soul, it stay my own. (*Beat.*) But you Marl…you held this too close to the rest of you, and it swallowin' you whole. You got to get outta here. Jim or no Jim. Find some soul to keep for yourself… somewheres out there.

*(**SANDY** caresses **MARLA**'s hair.)*

REE ANN. That Mr. Brown Marl. He leavin' for the north. In the mornin'.

*(**MARLA** looks at **REE ANN.** Then to **SANDY.**)*

MARLA. Thinkin' he'll let me go with him?

REE ANN. I'm thankin' he better.

(Lights crossfade to Nellie's boudoir.)

*(**NA ROSE** rubs **NELLIE**'s hands with lotion... calmly.)*

NELLIE. You know what been on me a lot lately, Rose?

NA ROSE. What's that Ainee?

NELLIE. That jukebox. The fella who sold it to Rollo. One what lost his wife... Done put his haunts into that box and now that box done brought 'em into this house. *(Beat.)* I got 'em in me now, I thank.

NA ROSE. Whatcha mean Ainee?

NELLIE. Got a lot on me can't shake. Like that Marla. Just...wonders 'bout her. Seem like her and me gon' always have friction. Like two pieces of cheap fabric that shoulda been silk but done got worn raggedy... rubbin' 'gainst each other...steady remindin' us how uncomfortable it is to be of so lil' value. *(Beat.)* I can't make it right for her. Her kinda pain I know too well. And the healin' ain't in this house. Rollo neither. He ready to shake up the soil and I'm ready to be planted in it. *(Beat.)* But you Rose, you the one I can make it right for. Gots to.

NA ROSE. I'm alright Ainee –

NELLIE. No. You ain't. *(Pause.)* You love that Mr. Brown, Rose. I saw your eyes tell me so. He ready to build you a new world. And I thankin', he might be capable.

(NA ROSE is lost for words. NELLIE looks at her earnestly.)

You the one I can make it right for, Rose. And I'm gonna. *(Beat.)* Now get on to bed with the gals.

NA ROSE. Turnin' in, Ainee?

NELLIE. Gonna go sit and wait.

NA ROSE. Ainee –

NELLIE. 'Nite Rose sugar.

(NA ROSE looks at AINEE with concern.)

(Lights fade on the boudoir.)

Scene Six

(Near daybreak. The room stay still. Dark. Hollow. Only a peek of moonlight washes into the yard.)

(The sound of the wind picks up outside.)

(A sodapop can breezes into the yard.)

(NELLIE *sits in the common room in her housecoat. Rocking in her chair; a rifle in her lap.)*

(TOM JR. *enters. He is drunk. He wobbles and sways into the yard. He carries a can of gasoline in his hands. He knocks at the side door.)*

(Silence.)

(He knocks again, louder.)

(NELLIE *carries the rifle in her arms and walks over to the door.)*

(TOM JR. *tries to peer inside the door.)*

TOM JR. Hello? Anyone thar?

> **(NELLIE** *sets the rifle by the door and appears in the screen.)*

NELLIE. Mr. Tom. You alright out there? It's the wee hours of the morn.

TOM JR. *(Slurring a bit.)* Miss Nellie. I... I needs to...talk witcha...

NELLIE. Mr. Tom, why don't you go'on home and git you some rest, and we can talk later in the full mornin'.

TOM JR. No, now, Miss Nellie. You gots somebody up in there I need to see.

NELLIE. I'm not sho' what somebody you mean, but there's nothin' but me and my gals here right now, and they's restin'.

TOM JR. No *(Hiccups.)* ...I'm talkin' 'bout that Negro man you got stayin' there. He fittin' the description of that... that outside agitator we's lookin' for...pull my own gun on me, he did...

NELLIE. Mr. Tom, you must be mistaken. Ain't no agitators here.

*(***TOM JR.*** *leans against the door pitifully.)*

TOM JR. Miss Nellie, I don't wants to hurt ya...

NELLIE. And I don't wants you hurt none either, Mr. Tom. Thas why I'm askin' ya kindly. Go on home. You come on by with your paw tomorrow, and we can do all the talkin' ya like.

TOM JR. I likes you, Miss Nellie. I swears I do. I'm a good man.

NELLIE. I know, Mr. Tom. I likes you too.

TOM JR. Please don't make me keep askin'. I needs to see that votin' Negro man you gots in there. Matter fact, you just send him out here with me, Miss Nellie. You ain't...you ain't even got to...let me in. Just send him on out here and we be square.

NELLIE. Can't do that, Mr. Tom.

TOM JR. There's...there's a mob at the highway...can't go nowhere. I just wants to...talk to 'im...'fore that mob finds you. I ain't tole nobody what I seen yet, Miss Nellie. I just wants to...deal with him myself...proper-like...

NELLIE. Like I say, can't do that, Mr. Tom.

(**TOM JR**. *bangs on the side door – pushing it open.* **NELLIE** *grabs her rifle and cocks it. Moves onto the porch in defiance.* **TOM JR**. *backs away.*)

TOM JR. Now Miss Nellie, you put that thang down, now.

(*He opens the can of gasoline.*)

NELLIE. Mr. Tom, you put that can down, I put down my rifle.

(**TOM JR**. *hiccups and stumbles a bit. Drops of gasoline fall from the can unwillingly. Spill at* **NELLIE**'s *feet. Spill on* **TOM**'s *shirt.*)

TOM JR. I'm the sheriff's son, Nellie. Ya be bringin' a whole lotta trouble on yaself ya don't want. This here land you got. This fine house. Nice jukebox.

NELLIE. I done worked hard for it, Mr. Tom. That true. But I tell you, ain't none of that gonna matter if you keep spillin' that like you doin'. Cuz it's just gon' be you and me. That's what I'm tellin' you right now.

(**TOM JR**. *dances with the idea. He puts the gasoline down and kneels over painfully.*)

TOM JR. They hung Eli, Miss Nellie.

NELLIE. I know, Mr. Tom.

TOM JR. And I couldn't...couldn't stop it.

NELLIE. Me neither, Mr. Tom.

TOM JR. Could I?

(*Silence.*)

You ever seen a ghost, Miss Nellie?

NELLIE. Yes, Mr. Tom. I has.

TOM JR. I seen one too. That night I saw your Na Rose.

I seen her lookin' like my Mayleen and I like to choke. Wanted me another chance to tell her I loved her. I never did tell her, Miss Nellie. Wanted to and just... never...had the guts...

(**TOM JR.** *swallows tears in his throat.* **NELLIE** *watches him for a moment. A decision: she sets her rifle down slowly.*)

NELLIE. Look Mr. Tom...look here... I'm puttin' my rifle down, see? I'm puttin' it down so's you can see...we friends here. I know, Mr. Tom, 'bout them ghosts. Gots my own haunts. They live in ya. Make you 'member all the horrible you done did to folks. All the horrible folks done did to you while you was figurin' out ya color and how you gon' surivive ya own skin. Them ghosts, they don't go away. You gots to absolve 'em. Make somethin' right. Thas what you got to do.

TOM JR. I always believed we could be friends, Miss Nellie. Whites and Coloreds – Negroes. I did. I never wanted no parts of this...separatin'. But here...ya got to follow rules you ain't never want ta'. Follow 'til you either start believin' in 'em, or you make yourself good n' mad.

(**NELLIE** *watches* **TOM JR.** *cautiously. Beat.*)

NELLIE. Mr. Tom, they's bringin' change here to Natchez. New day comin' if you can get on board with it. I know 'bout them rules. Been followin' so long, be too inconvenient to go another way. But it's comin', ready or not. And you can be part of that. Be part of the new day.

(*Beat.*)

TOM JR. In another world, Miss Nellie... But there's just no...fixin' this one...

(*Beat.* **TOM JR.** *pulls out a book of matches.*)

NELLIE. Mr. Tom!

(**NELLIE** *begins coughing furiously.*)

TOM JR. *(Continued.)* Not this one...

(**TOM JR.** *lights the match.*)

(Lights.)

(Flicker.)

(Flames.)

(Blackout.)

Epilogue

(Smoke and chaos. A gray darkness. Murmurs of troubled voices hum in the night. Above the hush, a blues riff sings higher than it all. It is **NA ROSE***'s voice. Something of a melody and a wail. A scream of grief. Smoke overwhelms the stage.)*

(Offstage voices in chaos. Through it all:)

*(***NA ROSE*** wails a blues riff.)*

(Lights of fire and smoke. Sounds of water splashing against it.)

VOICES. Oh God – Somebody help! – It's a fire! – Move to the yard – Ainee! – The whole front room! – Lord – Nellie! – Mr. Tom?! – They gone! – Mobs is comin' – The whole front room! – Somebody put it out! – Fetch some water quick!! – Marla! Sandy! – Ree Ann! Na Rose! – Rollo's truck – Get to the truck! – It's still goin'! – Got to move! – Ladies let's go – No time – Stay back – Sweet Jesus Lord GOD!!!!! –

(Lights rise on the common room.)

(Low and contained flames of fire continue to dance in the background. The rest of the fire has been quelled.)

(The common room is charred. Dust and smoke overwhelm the space. The only beautiful thing that remains is the jukebox. It glistens with an incomprehensible shine.)

*(***NA ROSE*** runs into the yard.)*

NA ROSE. No!!!

(The gals are on her heels.)

(They all stand before the remains of the common room, horrified.)

SANDY. She...

REE ANN.	**MARLA.**
God...	Lawd a-mighty.

(Headlights beam onto the stage and crossfade into an ominous light on ROLLO – frantic and hasty.)

ROLLO. We...we gots to get on the road. Mobs be comin' soon.

NA ROSE. Ainee...

(All stand motionless. OSSIE enters in haste, his clothes dusty with soot.)

OSSIE. Doused the last of it much as I could. No time left.

ROLLO. *(Choked.)* Yeah... *(Quick beat.)* Best git in that truck now. Sandy and Lil' Bit, ride in the hatch...rest... squeeze inside. *(Beat.)* Now I say!

(The gals follow ROLLO toward the truck. REE ANN stops.)

REE ANN. I stay.

MARLA. Ree Ann, you ain't comin'?

REE ANN. I stay. Natchez my home.

SANDY. Ree Ann! –

REE ANN. I go next door. Sleep for the night. But I stay here. On the land.

MARLA. You sho'?

REE ANN. No time for that. Go!

(**REE ANN** *nods urgently. They try to embrace her.*)

(*She pushes them and they painfully run off to the truck. She turns and heads off in the opposite direction.*)

(**NA ROSE** *hesitates a beat, and then rushes to the house.* **OSSIE** *grabs her.*)

NA ROSE. Ainee!

OSSIE. No Rose!

NA ROSE. I can't leave her!

OSSIE. She gone, Rose.

NA ROSE. *(Half talking / half singing.)* I only just seen her. She come to me in my dream last night. In a blues riff. Come and say – *Follow* it, Rose. Ya heart. *Hear ya blues* callin' Rose...and *follow it...*

OSSIE. Paradise Valley. Up north. Can take your blues with you.

(**ROLLO** *rushes back on.*)

ROLLO. Lil' Bit, we got to go'on now. No time to mourn. She... *(Bites back a wail.)* she gone. We got to move...

(**NA ROSE** *heads toward the truck, behind* **ROLLO** *and* **OSSIE**.)

(*She stops for a moment. Looks back at the house.*)

(*Suddenly, a white light washes over the jukebox.*)

(*An ominous light appears over* **NELLIE**. *She sits in her rocking chair, swaying to and fro.*)

NELLIE. *(Softly.)* You the one I can make it right for, Rose. And I'm gonna...

> *(The sound of a truck begins. NA ROSE looks after it...then runs toward it.)*
>
> *(Lights crossfade to a bright spotlight on the jukebox. It glistens and shines amidst the chaos.)*
>
> *(The unplugged cord lay visible.)*
>
> *(Softly at first, a blues riff plays from the jukebox. Howlin' Wolf, "Natchez Burnin'."*)*
>
> (**NELLIE** *rocks in her chair, listening. Lights fade on* **NELLIE** *and the jukebox.)*

End of Play

---

* A license to produce *Follow Me to Nellie's* does not include a performance license for "Natchez Burnin'." The publisher and author suggest that the licensee contact ASCAP or BMI to ascertain the music publisher and contact such music publisher to license or acquire permission for performance of the song. If a license or permission is unattainable for "Natchez Burnin'," the licensee may not use the song in *Follow Me to Nellie's* but should create an original composition in a similar style or use a similar song in the public domain. For further information, please see the Music and Third Party Materials Use Note on page iii.